Erle Stanley Gardner and The Murder Room

>>> This title is part of The Murder Room, our series dedicated to making available out-of-print or hard-to-find titles by classic crime writers.

Crime fiction has always held up a mirror to society. The Victorians were fascinated by sensational murder and the emerging science of detection; now we are obsessed with the forensic detail of violent death. And no other genre has so captivated and enthralled readers.

Vast troves of classic crime writing have for a long time been unavailable to all but the most dedicated frequenters of second-hand bookshops. The advent of digital publishing means that we are now able to bring you the backlists of a huge range of titles by classic and contemporary crime writers, some of which have been out of print for decades.

From the genteel amateur private eyes of the Golden Age and the femmes fatales of pulp fiction, to the morally ambiguous hard-boiled detectives of mid twentieth-century America and their descendants who walk our twenty-first century streets, The Murder Room has it all. >>>

The Murder Room
Where Criminal Minds Meet

themurderroom.com

Erle Stanley Gardner (1889–1970)

Born in Malden, Massachusetts, Erle Stanley Gardner left school in 1909 and attended Valparaiso University School of Law in Indiana for just one month before he was suspended for focusing more on his hobby of boxing than his academic studies. Soon after, he settled in California, where he taught himself the law and passed the state bar exam in 1911. The practise of law never held much interest for him, however, apart from as it pertained to trial strategy, and in his spare time he began to write for the pulp magazines that gave Dashiell Hammett and Raymond Chandler their start. Not long after the publication of his first novel, *The Case of the Velvet Claws*, featuring Perry Mason, he gave up his legal practice to write full time. He had one daughter, Grace, with his first wife, Natalie, from whom he later separated. In 1968 Gardner married his long-term secretary, Agnes Jean Bethell, whom he professed to be the real 'Della Street', Perry Mason's sole (although unacknowledged) love interest. He was one of the most successful authors of all time and at the time of his death, in Temecula, California in 1970, is said to have had 135 million copies of his books in print in America alone.

By Erle Stanley Gardner
(titles below include only those published in the Murder Room)

Perry Mason series

The Case of the Sulky Girl (1933)
The Case of the Baited Hook (1940)
The Case of the Borrowed Brunette (1946)
The Case of the Lonely Heiress (1948)
The Case of the Negligent Nymph (1950)
The Case of the Moth-Eaten Mink (1952)
The Case of the Glamorous Ghost (1955)
The Case of the Terrified Typist (1956)
The Case of the Gilded Lily (1956)
The Case of the Lucky Loser (1957)
The Case of the Long-Legged Models (1958)
The Case of the Deadly Toy (1959)
The Case of the Singing Skirt (1959)
The Case of the Duplicate Daughter (1960)

The Case of the Blonde Bonanza (1962)

Cool and Lam series

The Bigger They Come (1939)
Turn on the Heat (1940)
Gold Comes in Bricks (1940)
Spill the Jackpot (1941)
Double or Quits (1941)
Owls Don't Blink (1942)
Bats Fly at Dusk (1942)
Cats Prowl at Night (1943)
Crows Can't Count (1946)
Fools Die on Friday (1947)
Bedrooms Have Windows (1949)
Some Women Won't Wait (1953)
Beware the Curves (1956)
You Can Die Laughing (1957)
Some Slips Don't Show (1957)
The Count of Nine (1958)
Pass the Gravy (1959)
Kept Women Can't Quit (1960)
Bachelors Get Lonely (1961)
Shills Can't Cash Chips (1961)
Try Anything Once (1962)
Fish or Cut Bait (1963)
Up For Grabs (1964)

Cut Thin to Win (1965)
Widows Wear Weeds (1966)
Traps Need Fresh Bait (1967)
All Grass Isn't Green (1970)

Doug Selby D.A. series

The D.A. Calls it Murder (1937)
The D.A. Holds a Candle (1938)
The D.A. Draws a Circle (1939)
The D.A. Goes to Trial (1940)
The D.A. Cooks a Goose (1942)
The D.A. Calls a Turn (1944)
The D.A. Takes a Chance
  (1946)
The D.A. Breaks an Egg
  (1949)

Terry Clane series

Murder Up My Sleeve (1937)
The Case of the Backward
  Mule (1946)

Gramp Wiggins series

The Case of the Turning Tide
  (1941)
The Case of the Smoking
  Chimney (1943)

Two Clues (two novellas) (1947)

Try Anything Once

Erle Stanley Gardner

An Orion book

Copyright © The Erle Stanley Gardner Trust 1962

This edition published by
The Orion Publishing Group Ltd
Orion House
5 Upper St Martin's Lane
London WC2H 9EA

An Hachette UK company
A CIP catalogue record for this book is available from the British Library

ISBN 978 1 4719 0916 0

www.orionbooks.co.uk

CHAPTER 1

THE man who was pacing Bertha Cool's office was in such an ecstasy of self-pity that he barely noticed me when I entered the room.

"What a fool I was," he said. "What this is going to do to my wife, to my social position, to my job! It's terrible! It's unthinkable. It's——"

Bertha Cool interrupted him to say, "Here's Donald Lam now, Mr. Allen."

He looked at me, nodded and went on talking—not to anyone in particular.

"Looking back on what happened in the light of day it seems absolutely impossible that any man in his right mind could do these things. I must have had some sort of a mental lapse, Mrs. Cool."

Bertha shifted her hundred and sixty-five pounds in the big swivel chair. Her diamonds glittered as she gestured with her left hand. "Sit down. Take a load off your feet. This is the partner I was telling you about—Donald Lam. He can help you."

"I'm afraid no one can help me," Allen said. "The fat's in the fire. The——"

"What's it all about?" I asked him, breaking in on his hymn of lament.

"An indiscretion," he said, "that has pyramided into catastrophic proportions and now has become something that's going to affect my entire life. This is the one thing Dawn won't stand for."

"Who's Dawn?" I asked.

"My wife," he said.

"Sit down, sit down," Bertha Cool said. "For God's

sake, quit wearing out the rug and tell Donald what it's all about. Donald can't help you if you won't light."

Allen seated himself but couldn't seem to get his mind on anything except the disastrous cataclysm he felt was about to engulf him. He said, "It's so unlike me to do this sort of thing. I——"

Bertha Cool, turning to me, answered my question. "He took a chippy to a motel."

"No, no, no!" Allen said. "She wasn't a chippy. At least spare me *that*, Mrs. Cool."

"Well, what was she?"

"She's a very nice young lady. Good-looking, tolerant, broadminded; modern in every sense of the word, but definitely not common, and certainly not one who would consider a financial transaction in connection with her . . . her indiscretions."

"What motel?" I asked.

"The Bide-a-wee-bit," Bertha said.

"One of those places that rents rooms by the hour?" I asked.

"Heavens, no! This is a nice motel. High-class. Swimming pool. Very fine rooms. Telephones in each room. Bellboy service. Television. Central air conditioning with individual regulation by thermostat."

"How'd you happen to go *there*?" I asked.

"She suggested it. She'd been there before at a convention."

"So you took this girl there."

"Well, it wasn't—— It wasn't like that at all, Mr. Lam. I wish you'd try to understand."

"Hell!" Bertha exclaimed impatiently. "He's trying to understand but you won't tell him."

"Tell me about the girl," I said. "How did you meet her? How long had you known her?"

"I've known her for months."

"Intimately?"

"No, no, no! I do wish you'd try to understand, Mr. Lam."

Bertha sucked in her breath, started to say something, changed her mind. Her eyes were glittering with annoyance.

I gestured her to silence.

"Sharon," he said, "Miss Barker . . . is the hostess at a cocktail lounge where I occasionally have a drink."

"What do you mean, a hostess?"

"Well, sort of a head waitress. She seats people and takes reservations and assigns waitresses and sees that you get what you want, and then she keeps an eye on things."

"All right," I said, "you took her to this motel and I take it you got caught."

"No, no, you don't understand, Mr. Lam. It wasn't like that at all. I'm afraid that . . . well, the whole thing may result in very great complications. I need to have someone who can take the load off my shoulders. I'm not going to sit back and take it without a fight, I can promise you that."

"Now you're talking," I told him. "What did you have in mind?"

"Well, I want someone to——"

"You'd better tell him what happened and how it happened," Bertha Cool said. "Then you can talk about how you're going to start fighting."

Allen said, "I like women, Mr. Lam. I am not a libertine but I am deeply appreciative of feminine charm."

"Sharon is good-looking?" I asked.

"Wonderfully good-looking. Poised, cool, competent and the way she walks—there's a certain . . ."

"Wiggle," Bertha Cool interposed.

"No, no, not a wiggle! It's a sway, a rhythm, an undulating something. It's as though the girl were swimming."

'Go on," I said.

"Well, I like to compliment women on their appearance. When I like women, I—— It's my nature. I just can't resist it, Mr. Lam. If a woman has a dress that sets off her figure to advantage, or a color scheme that is very flattering—well, I comment on it."

"And their figures?" I asked.

"Their figures, yes."

"And legs," Bertha Cool commented dryly.

"Well . . . I notice them," Allen agreed.

"All right," I said, "you started complimenting Sharon Barker about her walk and——"

"No, no, nothing that crude. I commented on the dress she was wearing and the way she did her hair. And she has beautiful hands—very expressive, with long fingers. She uses them so wonderfully well! I—— Well, I complimented her on this and that."

"And these and those," Bertha Cool added.

"And one thing led to another and finally she would come and sit at my table for a little while, and we'd swap laughs and that was all there was to it."

"But you wound up in a motel," I said.

"Well, that was this one night."

"What happened?"

"I'd been working late at the office and my wife was spending the week-end in Reno with her mother. She makes a visit home about twice a year and I was pretty much at loose ends."

"So you dropped in at this cocktail bar."

"Yes."

"And it was late?"

"Yes."

'And business was slack?"

"Reasonably so."

"And Sharon came and sat at your table."

"Yes."

"And you got to talking to her about her work and her

4

ambitions and her appearance and told her she really should be on the screen. And then you mentioned her walk."

"Yes, yes, yes," he said. "How do you know all this, Mr. Lam?"

"I'm just following your lead," I said.

"Well, that's generally what happened, and it turned out that she didn't eat until after she got off work."

"Which was when?"

"Eleven o'clock at night. She eats very lightly during the first part of the evening and then, after she goes off work, has a good meal."

"So you invited her to go to dinner with you after eleven."

"Yes."

"And where did you go?"

"To some restaurant that specializes in goulash, some Hungarian place that she knew about."

"So she was known at the restaurant?"

"Yes."

"Were you known?"

"No."

"Had you been there before?"

"No."

"All right, you started to drive her home."

"She had her own car."

"You started out with two cars?"

"No, I had driven her to the restaurant and we started home—that is, I started back to the parking lot near the cocktail lounge where she had her car—and I drove around a bit and we were up on Mulholland Drive where we could look down and see the lights of the city, and so I stopped the car and . . . well, I put my arm around her and she snuggled up to me, and then I said something and she turned and tilted her face up and—well, I kissed her. It seemed the most natural thing in the world."

"And then what?"

"Well, that was all for a little while and then we kissed again and then we really started kissing, and the first thing I knew things had swept out of control and—well, she had been talking about this Bide-a-wee-bit Motel and what a nice place it was, and it wasn't too far away, so I just drove there and—when she saw where I was stopping she didn't make any protest and—well, suddenly I realized I had to go through with it."

"You registered?"

"She was very tactful. She told me that she'd do the registering if I'd give her money to pay for the room."

"She didn't make any token protest about registering as man and wife?"

"No. You see, by that time we were . . . well, we were just all wrapped up in each other. She hurried into the motel and——"

"You gave her some money?"

"Yes."

"How much?"

"Twenty dollars."

"How much was the room?" I asked.

"Thirteen dollars."

"She gave you back the seven dollars change?"

"Yes, yes, of course. My heavens, Mr. Lam, I wish you'd see this in its proper perspective. There was no financial consideration. That would have tainted the whole affair."

"I'm trying to get the proper perspective," I told him. "Then what happened?"

"What would *you* think?" Bertha asked.

Allen said, "Well, she came back and told me that she had told the clerk at the desk that she and her husband had been driving from San Francisco and were terribly tired and wanted a good quiet room and that she had registered and there wasn't the slightest question or suspicion."

"Under what name did she register?"

"The name of Carleton Blewett."

"And how did she happen to pick that name?"

"Well, that's sort of—that's a story in itself. She said she had heard that name once and it had made an impression on her mind. She had associated the name with San Francisco and since she was registering as having come from San Francisco, her mind sort of brought up the name of Carleton Blewett and she had registered that way."

"And the license number of the automobile?" I asked. "They usually ask for that in motels."

Allen said, "She played that one real cute. She hadn't thought about that, so when they handed back the registration blank and pointed out that she hadn't filled in the number, she was about to make up one, then she looked out the door and a car was being parked in front of the office and she just copied down that license number, simply changing the letter."

"When was all this?" I asked.

"Saturday."

"You mean this last Saturday—the day before yesterday?"

"Yes."

"All right," I said. "This young woman came back and told you you were Mr. Carleton Blewett and she was Mrs. Carleton Blewett and you found the unit to which you had been assigned. Then what?"

"We didn't find the unit. A bellboy took us to it."

"Okay, the bellboy took you there and you tipped him."

"Yes."

"How much?"

"A dollar."

"You didn't have any baggage?"

"No."

7

"Did the bellboy know that?"

"No. I told him I'd get the baggage out of the trunk myself, that we just wanted him to show us the unit."

"And you think that fooled the bellboy?"

"Well, he didn't act as though it were anything unusual."

"He wouldn't," I said. "Go on, then what happened? You got in the motel and I take it you got caught some way."

"No, we didn't, but—— Oh, this is terrible. This thing is going to ruin me. This——"

"Shut up!" Bertha Cool said. "Quit talking about that stuff and tell Donald what it is you want. Get down to cases."

"Well, I want *you* to be Mr. Blewett."

"Wait a minute," I said. "You want *me* to be Mr. Blewett?"

"Yes."

"How come?"

"I want you to go there with Sharon and be Mr. Blewett."

"I'm to go there *with* Sharon Barker?"

"Yes."

"When?"

"Tonight. As soon as possible."

"What does Sharon have to say about this?"

"She's a good scout. She appreciates the position I'm in. She'll co-operate."

"Just what position are you in?"

"Well, it's a peculiar story. You see, actually, Mr. Lam, nothing happened there at the motel."

"What do you mean, nothing happened?"

"We got in an argument."

"Over what?"

"To tell you the truth, I don't know. I had made the mistake of picking up a bottle of whiskey and we had

8

setups sent to the room and started drinking and I started —well, pawing, is the way she expressed it, and—somehow it didn't go across the way it had up there in the car. It wasn't spontaneous and natural and—well, dammit, it just didn't seem the right thing to do. She said something about how she hated to be pawed over. She said she didn't mind sex as long as it was frank and open, but she hated this pawing business and—well, she slapped me, and I got mad and she got up and walked out. I waited for her to come back. She never did come back. I found out afterwards she had called a taxi and went home."

"So what did you do?"

"I waited awhile and must have gone to sleep. Then I woke up and was good and mad. I got in my car and drove home."

"Then what's all the excitement about?"

"The murder," he said.

"What murder?"

Bertha Cool said, "That was last Saturday, the night Ronley Fisher was murdered."

"The guy who was hit over the head and dumped in the swimming pool?" I asked.

Bertha nodded.

I thought for a moment and said, "That was at a motel somewhere in that general vicinity, wasn't it?"

Allen said, "That's right. They didn't mention the name of the motel in the papers. They referred to it as one of the swanky motels. But one of the papers did publish the name. . . . That's newspaper policy. When you have suicides or murders in a public place, the newspapers don't mention the name of the place as a rule, they just say it was a downtown hotel, and they're doing the same thing with the better class of motels."

I turned to Allen. "All right," I said, "now, what happened?"

"Well the police are anxious to talk with anyone who

was in that wing of the motel. They thought that they might learn something. The murder is one of those things that simply has to be solved. Ronley Fisher was the deputy district attorney trying a big murder case. His death may have been accidental. The swimming pool was drained of water that night. They change the water once a week. Fisher could have been a little high and decided to jump into the pool and smashed his head on the cement floor, or he could have been hit over the head and then dropped into the empty pool.

"If it's an accident, there are lots of things to be explained. If it's a murder, the police *have* to solve it.

"Here's an article in yesterday's paper. It says the police have obtained the names of every person staying in the motel that night and are engaged in running them down, interrogating them to see whether they saw anything unusual. Some of the people are as far away as New York, but they're covering all of them."

"I see," I said. "And so the police are going to be looking for a Mr. and Mrs. Carleton Blewett at the San Francisco address, and then find the San Francisco address was a phony."

"Exactly," he said, hanging his head.

"All right, now what is it you want?"

"I want you to go there tonight with Sharon Barker. I called the motel, told them I was Carleton Blewett, that we were keeping the unit but were going to make a quick trip to San Diego. I sent them twenty-six dollars by messenger. So the unit will be kept on the occupied list and since the police will be advised that the occupants are returning they won't be too worked up about that phony address in San Francisco. They'll figure we're just a couple on a good-time trip.

"So you and Sharon can go back there. Sharon will go into the office and ask for the key, and the clerk at the desk will remember her. In any event, the clerk will have reported my phone conversation to the police and they'll be there to interview you."

"So then what happens?"

Allen said, "It's a perfect setup. The police aren't going to get mad about a week-end party. They only want to be sure they've found the couple who were there Saturday night. You tell them you and Sharon had a spat that night and that she ran out on you, that she's making it up to you now."

I shook my head. "No dice," I said.

"What do you mean, no dice?"

"I mean I wouldn't touch it with a ten-foot pole."

"Look," Allen said, "I'm not unaware of the grave responsibilities of the situation. I have told Mrs. Cool I would pay one thousand dollars to have you impersonate me for this one night and tell the police that you know nothing and saw nothing on Saturday night, and that will be the truth because I didn't see anything and—— Don't you understand? The police don't really expect anyone did, it's simply a gesture they're making of rounding up *everyone* who was at the motel. I can't afford to have them find me."

"Who are you?" I asked.

"I'm Carleton Allen."

"What's your line of business?"

"I'm in the investment business."

"Go to the police," I said. "Offer to tell them your story on the quiet. Let them interview you and let them interview Sharon and that's all there will be to it. They won't divulge your secret. They're after information, that's all."

He shook his head violently and said, "The situation is complicated. I've offered a thousand, Mr. Lam. I'll make it fifteen hundred."

Bertha snapped bolt upright in her chair, her greedy eyes glittering.

"What's the catch?" I asked. "Why can't you go to them and tell them the true story right from the start?"

"My wife," he said.

"What about your wife?"

"My wife is Dawn Getchell."

"Dawn Getchell," I said, "I don't . . ." Suddenly I broke off.

"My God," Bertha said, "you mean she's Marvin Getchell's daughter?"

"Yes," he said.

"Getchell, with all of his millions, can fix things up for you," Bertha said. "He could——"

"He could cut my throat," Allen interrupted. "He doesn't like me and never has and—this would finish our marriage. . . . Oh, why did I ever get myself in such a jam? This is the damnedest thing I've ever done. I've been in scrapes before but this is a lulu! This is the pay-off!"

I shook my head, said to Bertha, "We can't touch it."

"Now look," Bertha said, "you're ingenious, Donald. You can always find some way to do things if you want to bad enough."

"This one I don't want to do," I said.

Bertha glared at me.

I started to walk out.

Carleton Allen said, 'No, no, wait. Now, there must be *some* way."

I said, "Why did you bring this deal to us, Allen?"

He said, "You're the only one Sharon will work with."

"Sharon knows *me*?" I asked.

"You were pointed out to her."

"When?"

"When you were in the cocktail lounge."

"So Sharon is the hostess in the Cock and Thistle."

"Right."

I said, "We still can't do it."

12

Bertha said, "Why don't you take a walk, Allen? Go out in the outer office for about five minutes and let me talk it over with Donald."

I told her, 'It won't do any good, Bertha, I . . ."

Allen jumped to his feet with alacrity. "I'll be back in five minutes," he said, and shot out the door.

Bertha glared daggers at me. "Fifteen hundred dollars for a night's work and you kick it out the window," she said. "In addition to that, I'll bet this girl is a dish and——"

"Look," I told Bertha, "this is a red-hot murder case. We're being called onto act as red herrings and throw the police off the real scent. In the second place, we're putting ourselves completely in the power of this Sharon Barker. Any time she wants to squeal to the cops she can have our license. Now then, do you want to live your life knowing that any time some cocktail hostess decides to blow the whistle you're going to be put out of business?"

Bertha blinked her eyes, thinking that over.

"Why so conservative?" she asked. "You have often told me that you will try anything once. Why not give this a try?"

I shook my head. "Carleton Allen," I said, "may be Dawn Getchell's husband but the guy's a heel. What's more, he isn't telling us all of the background—just enough to sucker us in."

Bertha sighed, picked up the telephone, said to the receptionist, "This fellow, Allen, out there waiting—tell him to come back in."

Allen jerked the door open as soon as he had the message, looked expectantly at Bertha Cool, then, at what he saw in her face, turned to me and again started feeling sorry for himself.

He closed the door, slumped down in a chair and said, "I can see the answer in your faces. *Why* can't you give me a break?"

"Because," I said, "we can't afford to get that far out on a limb."

"Look, Lam," he said, "this is a very serious matter. It isn't generally known, but my wife doesn't have long to live. I'm in line to inherit something like twenty million dollars. Look, Lam, if you'll ride along on this I'll see that your agency gets all the high-class business it can handle."

Bertha's chair squeaked as she shifted her weight and looked at me.

I said, "I'll tell you what I'll do, Allen. I'll think your proposition over. If I play it, I'll play it my way, not yours. So let's get things straight at the start. Now, as I understand it, all you want is to have the police fail to tag you as Carleton Blewett. Is that right?"

"Yes. I want them to feel that they have checked Carleton Blewett and his wife and wiped them off the books."

"And if I can do that, no matter *how* it's done, that's okay by you?"

"Oh, Lam," he said jumping to his feet, "that would be a lifesaver! You'd—— You have no idea what it would mean to me. It would give me a new lease on life."

I said, "You've talked this over with Sharon Barker?"

"Yes."

"Get her on the telephone," I said. "I want to talk with her."

He whipped a little black book out of his pocket. Bertha spun the dial to clear him on an outside line, and Allen's stubby, well-manicured fingers moved over the dial.

A moment later he said, "Hello. Sharon? Guess who this is . . . That's right. Look, I'm up at the office of those detectives, and Donald Lam wants to talk with you."

I took the phone as he extended it to me and said, "Hello, Sharon."

Her voice was cool, but seductive. "Hello, Donald."

"You understand the deal that's being put up to me?"

"Yes."

"You're willing to go through with it?"

"With you, I am. I'm not going to go through with it with just any man, but I'm willing to do it with you."

"Why me?"

"I saw you a week or so ago. You were in my place for cocktails with a young woman."

"You knew who I was?"

"Someone pointed you out to me as Donald Lam, the detective."

"That's bad."

"Why is it bad?"

"A detective tries to keep anonymous. He tries to look nondescript and doesn't want people to know who he is. He wants to blend into the background."

"Well," she said, "you didn't blend very well, Donald. I couldn't help watching you."

"Why?"

"Because you were such a gentleman."

"How come?"

"That girl who was with you was in love with you and you were a perfect gentleman, you didn't . . . oh, I don't know. You were considerate and . . . well, you were nice. You didn't play her for what you could get out of it—and you could have had it all.

"So when they asked me if I'd put on an act with a private detective, I said there was only one detective in the business I'd go for—and just so we don't get our wires crossed, Donald, this is business, you know."

"I know."

"There are twin beds in that room in the motel and they'll *both* be used and—well, you'll be a gentleman, that's all."

"I'll try."

"Okay by me. Do you want to drop around and talk things over?"

"What things?"

"Ground rules."

"Such as what?"

"Look, Donald, I'm not going to sit up all night and I'm not going to be arguing all night. Lights are off when I say put them off and that's that—well, you know."

"I'll drop around," I said.

"Alone," she told me.

"I'll see you later," I told her.

I hung up and turned to Allen.

I said, "We'll represent you for two thousand dollars and all the expenses. The expenses are going to be high. You want to see that you are not connected with the Carleton Blewett who registered at the Bide-a-wee-bit Motel the night Ronley Fisher was murdered. That's *all* you care about. You don't care *how* I go about it. Is that right?"

"That's right."

"Put it in writing," I said, and turned to Bertha. "Call in a stenographer and get it down in black and white and have him sign it," I said.

"Where are you going, Donald?"

"Out."

I started for the door, turned and said over my shoulder, "And be sure you get the two thousand dollars cash in advance as a retainer."

Bertha's face was a study of futile rage.

CHAPTER 2

ELSIE BRAND, my secretary, said, "What's giving with Bertha this morning?"

I grinned and said, "She has a man in there who's lower than a snake's belly. He's feeling sorry for himself in seventeen different languages including Scandinavian."

"And you're going to help him out?"

"Perhaps."

"Is it dangerous, Donald?"

"It depends," I said. "It's tied in with Ronley Fisher's death Saturday night, and I may have to spend the night with a beautiful siren, and I want your clip file on Fisher."

Her face flushed. "Donald!"

"Actually you got me this piece of business," I told her.

"How?"

"Do you remember when we went to the Cock and Thistle cocktail bar?"

"Yes. Why?"

"Someone saw us there and thought we made a nice couple."

Her face colored slightly.

"And decided I was a gentleman."

"Why, Donald?"

"I guess because I wasn't pawing."

"Would you paw in a cocktail lounge?"

"I guess some men do, but apparently I wasn't mentally pawing. This girl seems to have objections to people who paw."

"We all do."

"What's pawing?"

"Restless hands."

"You mean a man is supposed to keep his hands in his pockets when he's out with a girl?"

"No, of course not, but . . ."

"Well?" I asked.

"It all depends on the man," she said, "whether it's pawing or . . ."

"Or what?"

"Or a caress," she said, and instantly became all business. "I'll get you the clippings on the Ronley Fisher murder."

"All right," I said, "let's take a look."

As I studied the clippings in the envelope Elsie had brought for me I became convinced the police had absolutely nothing in the way of tangible clues, and yet they were dealing with a case which simply had to be solved.

Ronley Fisher had been a young deputy district attorney. He had been successful in a couple of big cases and had made quite a name for himself.

At the time of his death he was prosecuting Staunton Cliffs and Marilene Curtis for the murder of Cliffs's wife. Cliffs claimed the killing was accidental; that they had quarreled bitterly and his wife had brandished a .38-caliber revolver, menaced him with it and threatened to kill him; that he advanced to take the gun away from her; that she had fired one shot which had just nicked him in the arm; that he had grabbed for the gun and tried to twist it out of her hands and that as she struggled to break loose, he had twisted her arm; that the gun had accidentally been discharged as she put pressure on the trigger in twisting her arm.

Cliffs told the police a pretty convincing story until they started checking on clues and had made him admit that Marilene Curtis, his mistress, was in the house at the time of the shooting; that the quarrel had been over the fact that Cliffs wanted a divorce which his wife wouldn't give him. Police accused Cliffs of killing his wife in cold blood, then having Marilene turn the gun on him and carefully fire a bullet that would just crease his arm. It was at that stage of the inquiry that Cliffs stopped answering questions and sent for a lawyer.

Now, with Cliffs on trial, the death of Ronley Fisher was a dramatic development that was putting the police on the spot, selling newspapers and giving counsel for the defense a big break.

If Fisher's death had been accidental, it was a dramatic development in a red-hot case. If he had been murdered, the fat was in the fire, the police on a spot, and the motive for the murder something that was of the greatest importance to ascertain.

The facts in the case were simple and very meager.

About five o'clock Sunday morning a night watchman at the Bide-a-wee-bit Motel had noticed something in the swimming pool. He had investigated and found the body of a fully clothed man at the bottom of the pool.

Earlier, Saturday evening at ten-thirty, the pool had been drained and cleaned. At one o'clock the valves had been turned on, bringing in a flood of new water.

At three the pool had been fully filled and an automatic device turned the water off.

The watchman, having discovered the body, called the police and the so-called "security service" of the motel, actually a house detective named Donleavey Ralston, a former investigator for the district attorney's office who had quit his job under fire to engage in what he referred to as "private practice".

I digested the clippings. The more I saw of the case the less I liked any part of it.

CHAPTER 3

AT this time in the afternoon there was little activity at the cocktail bar. The cocktail hour rush hadn't started and the afternoon shopping and pickup trade had slackened off.

I entered the place and stood for a moment letting my eyes get accustomed to the dim light.

There was a light over the cash register and the bar was fairly well lit, but purple lights gave the impression of deep moonlight over the tables, and the booths along the edges were invisible to a man coming in from the lighted streets.

I didn't see her as she glided up beside me.

"Donald Lam," she said, and her voice was a purring caress.

"Sharon?" I asked.

"Yes. Want to talk ground rules?"

"Can I buy a drink?"

"You can't talk with me unless you do."

"Can I buy you one?"

"No. That's against the rules."

"Where do we talk?"

"Come with me."

She escorted me over to a booth in a far corner; a booth that was so arranged that it shut off the rest of the cocktail lounge.

"What do you want to drink, Donald?"

"A King Alphonse," I said.

"All right. I'll get it and bring it myself. Give me a dollar, Donald."

I gave her the dollar.

"The bartender is a good Joe," she said. "He'll take over and give me a signal if I have to be on the job. Just sit over there in the far corner and relax."

I settled down on the soft leather cushions and waited.

By the time Sharon was back with the King Alphonse, my eyes had become sufficiently accustomed to the dim light so I could make her out.

She was a slim, long-legged girl with neat curves and cool appraising eyes that were remarkably steady in their inspection.

She brought the King Alphonse on a tray, bent over to put it on the table, looked hastily back over her shoulder, then put the tray on a corner of the table and slid in next to me.

"Donald," she said, "I'm scared."

"How scared?" I asked.

"Nothing that a thousand dollars won't cure, but just the same, I'm frightened."

"Are you getting a grand out of this?" I asked.

She arched her penciled eyebrows. "Didn't you know that, Donald?"

I shook my head.

"Donald, what gives?"

"I don't know," I said, "other than a thousand dollars."

"Don't be like that."

"Like what?"

"Don't wisecrack when I'm asking for information."

"Suppose we start putting two and two together," I said. "Tell me a little more about why you picked me out as the one to build up the background."

"Because I like you. In this job a girl gets so she can size up men pretty darned well. You were in here a few nights ago with a girl. . . . Who was that girl, Donald?"

"Just a friend."

"She . . . she couldn't take her eyes off you, and you were such a gentleman; so nice, so considerate and—well, just so poised about the whole thing. . . . Tell me, Donald, is she somebody's wife? Was it that kind of an affair?"

I said, "We're supposed to talk about you."

"Well, I have to know something about you. After all," she said archly, "I'm supposed to spend the night with you."

"And you wanted to discuss the ground rules," I reminded her.

"That can come later," she said. "What I want to know now is how much of a chance I'm taking."

"That depends."

"On what?"

"On how much you know."

"Donald, I don't know a darned thing. I went into this motel, and the clerk looked me over pretty carefully. I understand the clerk has told police that he'll know me if he sees me again.

"Now, that's the thing that leaves me no choice in the matter because I can't give up my job here, and sooner or later they're going to find me and then it will be pretty darned difficult to explain what happened."

"And so?" I asked.

"So," she said, "with a grand to back me up in my determination, I'm going ahead with it."

"And just what is this *it* you're referring to?"

"Don't you know?"

"Only in a sketchy way. I'd rather have you tell me."

"All I know is that the police have tried to check on the registration, and the address didn't check out; that is, there's a house there and people there but they aren't the ones. They can prove that they were in San Francisco all Saturday and Sunday.

"Then they checked the license number of the automobile I'd written down, and they drew a blank there. That automobile was an Olds, and the car and owners were in Seattle all that week-end. So then the police knew they were dealing with a phony registration. I'd written the make of car on the registration as a Cadillac."

"Why a Cad?" I asked.

"Because that was the first car I happened to see when I looked up from the registration desk and out the window of the office. It was a Cadillac, and the license number was VGH 535. So I changed the G to a C and wrote the license as VCH 535."

"So the police knew it was a phony registration," I said. "Do you suppose they'll start trying to check on Cadillacs with license numbers that could have been transposed?"

"Not a chance," she said. "They'll think I just made the whole license number up—which I would have done if I hadn't just happened to look up and see this car among the four or five parked in front of the office."

"And so?" I asked. "Where do we go from here?"

"And so," she said, "I'm to go to the motel with you, go in and ask for the key. The clerk will have notified the police by this time that the couple who rented the unit had sent in money to pay for keeping it and will be back from San Diego to occupy it. We'll go to the room and have some drinks and the police will come. They'll question me and I've got to appear to be a fallen woman, and you've got to appear to be a sucker."

"You're willing to do that?"

"I'm willing to go that far," she said. "After all, people don't expect a hostess in a cocktail lounge to be a plaster saint. I've been around. I've been married and divorced and—well, I've been around."

"This won't affect your job in any way?"

"Heavens, no. The proprietor likes to have a hostess with a little aura of wickedness about her. That part of it's all right."

"What part isn't all right?"

"What the police are going to do."

"And what do you think they'll do?"

23

She said, "I'm going to tell them my story. I'm going to put it right on the line with them that I'm having an unmarried honeymoon with you."

"What's the real story?" I asked.

"The real story is that this man I was with, I've always known as Carleton."

"No last name?"

"No last name."

"How long have you known him?"

"I've seen him in here—oh, maybe a dozen times."

"You've been nice to him?"

"I would talk to him for a while, and a couple of times when business was dull I would sit at his table."

"Then what happened?"

"Well, this Saturday night he was on the loose and I could tell it. Don't ask me how. I just knew that he was on the loose almost as soon as I saw him here."

"That was a special occasion?"

"Of course it was a special occasion. I can tell you this much about him, Donald. The guy's married. His wife was out somewhere, away visiting friends or something, because you could just tell he was on the loose."

"And you?" I asked.

"All right," she said, "I was on the loose too. I'd been going with a guy up to about a month ago and then I'd thrown him over and—well, I didn't have anything to do —no place to go except my apartment and I was lonesome."

"And what happened?"

"Well, it started out just a little at a time. Carleton invited me to dinner. I felt that I'd go with him, have a couple of drinks and that would be all there'd be to it. That was what I had in mind."

"What did *he* have in mind?"

"Anything he could get, I guess. That's what they all have in mind. He was going to crowd his luck until he

24

ran into a sign saying road closed. What the hell did you expect?"

"I didn't expect," I said. "I was just asking you what you expected."

"All right, that's what I expected and that's the way the situation developed."

"And you went out to dinner with him?"

"Yes."

"And then what?"

"Well, he was going to drive me back to where my car was and he said he wanted to go up over Mulholland Drive on the way back and that was okay with me."

"You knew what it meant?"

"Good God, Donald, of course I knew what it meant. The guy was going to stop the car to quote look at the lights unquote, and then he was going to cuddle up a little bit and start necking and see how far he could go, and his hands were going to explore until they got stopped —if they ever did get stopped."

"And that was all right with you?"

"Of course it was all right with me. I'm human. I just intended to put up the no trespassing signs at the point I picked out, not the point he picked out."

"So what happened?"

"Well, we went up there and sat and looked at the lights and—believe it or not, Donald, the guy was real nice. He didn't try to be crude about things. He just sat and talked and looked at the lights and all of a sudden I realized I liked him."

"And then what?"

"He turned toward me to say something and I held my face at just the right angle so that he had a chance to lean forward and kiss me."

"And he leaned forward and kissed you?"

"Of course he did. What the hell? I'd opened the gate. The man wasn't made of wood."

"And then what?"

"Well, it was what happened afterward—or rather, what didn't happen afterward, that made it so nice. He didn't try to follow up on the advantage, rushing things along as though he had to get things over with in order to catch a train. We cuddled a bit and he kissed me some more and—well, I got feeling my oats and I gave him the full treatment."

"Then what happened?"

"Then," she said, "having let him get to first base I thought he'd try to steal second and I was willing to have him steal second, but that was as far as he was going to go."

"And?" I asked.

She said, "He was so darned nice. He didn't start pawing, he didn't try to do anything. He just started the car."

"And then what?"

"Well, I—well, you know how it is—well, perhaps you *wouldn't* know how it is, but I thought perhaps I wasn't doing so good. I had so convinced myself that I was going to have to put up the no trespassing signs that when he didn't start exploring to see where they were, I felt just a little . . ."

"Disappointed?" I asked.

She hesitated. "No, not disappointed," she said thoughtfully, "but I was doing just a little self-appraising and—— Well, frankly, Donald, that was the first time anything like that had ever happened to me."

"Go ahead," I said.

"So he drove along, just being as nice as could be and then all of a sudden he turned in at this motel. It was a motel we'd mentioned earlier when we were talking about an advertising convention I'd attended. I told him I'd been there at a cocktail party and had been in the pool, and what a nice place it was."

"And then what?"

"Well, when he swung in there, I recognized a real super approach—and somehow I liked it. It was so cool, so daring—and no questions.

"You know, Donald, there are some questions a girl hates. If a man suddenly says, 'Look, darling, will you go to a motel with me and register as man and wife?' there just isn't any good way of handling the situation. If you say 'No,' it may not be what you want to say, but you can't say 'Yes' without cheapening yourself all to hell.

"I may as well tell you right now, Donald, I hate to be pawed. I don't mind having men put their hands on me if they're nice about it. But some just paw and push and—I just don't like to be pawed, that's all."

"Anyway, you fell for this approach."

"I just said to myself, pretty smart, huh? This guy is really a smoothie. I bet he'll be interesting, and I'm lonely, so why not? I didn't make a scene."

"And then what?"

"He asked me just as nice as you please if I'd care to do the registering."

"So you went in and registered?"

"I went in and registered and told them my husband and I had driven down from San Francisco and were tired, and I thought the clerk looked me over a little bit. I had heard the name Carleton Blewett somewhere and it had stuck in my mind. I knew the man I was with as Carleton, and so I just registered as Mr. and Mrs. Carleton Blewett and made up a San Francisco address.

"Then we went to the motel unit, and the bellboy wanted to take the baggage out, but Carleton told him that he'd take it out later—and, well, that didn't fool the bellboy any. I know darned well the bellboy went back and reported to the desk that we didn't have any baggage."

"Then what?"

"Well then, after we got into the unit Carleton produced a bottle of whiskey. That's where he made his mistake and that's where I made my mistake. I'd been having champagne with the dinner. I really like champagne when it's good, and I like the things that go with champagne, the dim lights and the budding romance and all that."

"And you didn't like the whiskey?"

"No."

"And didn't drink it?"

"Not much of it. He telephoned for setups, and the man who brought them wasn't a bellboy. I don't think Carleton noticed it but I noticed it."

"You say it wasn't a bellboy?"

"No, it was the house detective."

"Do they have one in a motel?"

"They do in the Bide-a-wee-bit. That's quite a place, you know."

"I know. And what happened?"

"Well, he sized us up and went out and frankly I expected the phone to ring and someone to tell Carleton that his lease had expired; that there was no baggage in the room and they wanted the room vacated and he could get his money back at the desk after deductions for the linen and maid service."

"And so?"

"And so I stalled around awhile. I went to the bathroom and fixed my hair, and Carleton poured a couple of drinks and I told him I didn't want all of mine, so he drank his and then he drank mine, and then he fixed himself another one and all of a sudden I realized that he was mixing whiskey on top of champagne and it wasn't going so good. His face got a little loose and flabby and— it's hard to say, but all of a sudden the guy didn't look so good to me any more."

"And then?" I asked.

"Then," she said, "he made his mistake. He started pawing. That was the thing I'd liked about his approach

28

in the first place; it had been so smooth and so sophisticated and so—so cool. If he'd just kept on that plane in the room, things would have been okay, but he started going ahead on a take-it-for-granted basis, and all of a sudden I just got fed up and picked up my purse and walked out."

"What did you do?"

"Went to the phone booth, called a taxi and went home."

"Now, what are you going to tell the police?"

"I'm going to tell them the exact truth."

"And what are you going to tell them about Carleton Blewett?"

"You're going to be Carleton Blewett. Of course that's not your name, but I'm going to tell the police you were the man who was with me Saturday, that we had a tiff when you got swacked and I walked out on you. I'm going to say you rang up and apologized, that I accepted your apology and I'm making it up to you tonight for having been an old meanie and walking out on you Saturday night.

"You're going to have to take it from there, but there won't be much to take. All they'll want is to ask us if we saw anything of Ronley Fisher, what time we went to bed, whether we heard anything out of the usual and all that—and of course after the police leave we'll have to stay on all night so it won't look like a plant."

I said, "This house detective who brought in the setups will say, 'This isn't the guy who was with her.' "

"No, he won't. Carleton was on the bed. He kept his face turned away. That's one thing that soured the party. After we got into the motel he acted so furtive and ashamed of me."

"And then he came to you and offered you a grand to go to the police and tell them this story?" I asked.

"No, no. He didn't ever come to me. I haven't seen him

from that day to this, and I'll bet a hundred bucks I never see him again."

"Well, what about this grand?" I asked.

She said, "He told me over the telephone that the police would be looking for me and the police would probably find me because I was in the public eye, so to speak. Sooner or later the clerk or the bellboy would run onto me."

"So you were promised a thousand over the telephone?"

"Yes."

"Think you'll get it?"

"I've got it."

"You have it?"

"Why, yes. You didn't think I'd go this far without it, did you?"

"How did you get it?"

"A messenger brought me a package of nice neat hundred-dollar bills."

"And what did you tell Carleton over the telephone?"

"He said he wanted me to go back to the motel; that he'd notified the motel clerk to hold the unit and had send money by messenger. He said that I couldn't go back by myself; that he'd hire some private detective who would go with me and pose as the man in the case. The clerk could notify the police and they'd question us and I could tell my story, and that would be enough to get him off the hook."

"Why would it be enough to get him off the hook?"

"Because the bellboy or the house detective would support me that he was drunk and didn't know from straight up."

"And what did you tell him?"

"I told him nothing doing. That I wasn't that kind of a girl. He offered me five hundred and I told him nothing doing, and then I suddenly remembered about you and

I told him, all right, now look, Carleton, if you can get Donald Lam to go through with the thing with me and if you'll give me a thousand bucks, it's okay. Otherwise, no dice."

"And so?" I asked.

"So here you are," she said. "And Carleton has phoned the motel and told them to keep Unit 27 for him. They're holding it. Carleton never checked out."

I said, "The house detective saw Carleton. The bellboy saw him. Suppose the police ask them to look me over?"

"They didn't look him over Saturday night," she said. "The bellboy didn't care and the house detective looked *me* over."

"Did you look sexy?" I asked.

"Donald, I *always* look sexy. That's my job. What's the matter with your eyes? Or is it the light in here?"

"It's the light in here."

"Well, you'll see more of me later on," she said, and laughed.

I said, "I won't go for any lying in a big way, but on the theory that I had drinks and propositioned you and you accepted and we went to a motel, I'm willing to ride along. It *may* work, but not the way it was planned. The main thing is not to tell the police we have a sponsor."

Her face lit up. "You think we can get by playing it right across the board?"

"We can give it a whirl," I told her. "When do we start?"

"I get off work tonight at eleven and I like dinner afterwards. Are you going to buy me a dinner, Donald?"

"Sure."

"Okay," she said. "Do we want baggage, or no baggage?"

"It'll be better without baggage," I said. "Play it just the way you did Saturday night."

"Okay, Donald," she said. "I've got to get back to the

customers. See you at eleven. 'Bye now." She pressed her forefinger to her lips, then pressed the finger against my lips.

I waited about ten minutes, then walked out.

She had her back turned to me as I walked out, but she flashed me a quick smile over her shoulder. She was taking orders from a table with two couples. The place was beginning to fill up for the cocktail hour.

CHAPTER 4

I WAS at the cocktail lounge at eleven. Sharon kept me waiting about three minutes, then joined me and we went out to my car. We went to a Hungarian restaurant and had champagne. I gave the waitress a good tip and we started driving to the Bide-a-wee-bit Motel.

"Nervous?" I asked.

"Shivering," she said.

"Take it easy," I told her. "It'll be over soon and you'll have it all behind you."

"Aren't we going to stop?" she asked.

"Stop where?"

"Along the road?"

"What for?"

"Getting acquainted a little. It seems so cold and businesslike to go to a motel with a man you haven't even kissed . . ."

"It *is* cold and businesslike," I told her, "and you aren't going to have time to worry about reactions. The police will be there before you've finished your second drink."

"Whiskey on top of champagne?" she asked.

"Champagne on top of champagne," I told her. "I have some cold bottles packed in dry ice in a cardboard carton."

"I thought we weren't going to carry baggage."

"This isn't baggage. This is champagne."

"Glasses?" she asked. "I hate to drink champagne out of a tumbler."

"Of course there are glasses," I told her. "They're all chilled."

"Donald, you think of darned near everything," she said.

"Why the darned near?" I asked.

"You didn't think of my feelings—of . . . well, that a little warm-up would help."

"It might start something that would keep us from having our minds on the story we're going to tell the cops."

"Well, maybe we could finish . . ."

"What?" I asked.

"Nothing," she said.

I drove straight to the Bide-a-wee-bit Motel.

"All right," I said, "you've got to ask for the key. And remember, you're Mrs. Carleton Blewett now, but when the police come they'll ask for your driving license and then we give our real names."

"My God," she said, "I'm not dumb enough not to know what the score is."

She went into the motel, was gone about two minutes, then came back with a bellboy in tow.

The bellboy ran ahead of us to Unit 27 and stood by to take our baggage.

I let him take out the cardboard carton so he could be certain that was all the baggage we had. Then I gave him a dollar tip and we went inside.

Sharon looked around the room nervously, said, "I never felt so self-conscious!"

I opened the cardboard carton and took out a cold bottle of champagne. "This will help," I said.

"I feel that I hardly know you, Donald."

The champagne cork made a noise like a pistol shot, and Sharon gave a little squeal.

"Donald, you frighten me!"

I turned to look at her. She was straightening her stockings, showing lots of leg. "Oh," she said, keeping her skirt up, "I thought you had your back turned."

"I changed my stance," I told her.

"*You* would," she said, and smiled invitingly.

"Come on," I said, "and drink a toast to adventure."

I sat down in the overstuffed chair.

She came over to perch on the arm of the chair. I handed her an ice-cold champagne glass and filled the two glasses.

"To adventure!" I said.

We touched the brims of the glasses. Then we sat sipping champagne.

"Donald," she said at length, "do you suppose the police are coming right away?"

"That depends," I said, "on how far they want us to go before they break in. The clerk knew you?"

"Sure. What's more, the man who brought the drinks to us Saturday was there in the lobby. I could feel him looking me over when I had my back turned."

"Can you feel them when they look you over?" I asked.

"Some of them, yes. You can feel their eyes moving over every inch of you."

"Do you dislike that?"

"No, I like it. I've got lots of nice inches, Donald."

"I've noticed."

"You'll see that I know what I'm talking about, Donald. . . . How's the champagne doing?"

I filled her glass.

"You're nice," she said, running fingers through my hair.

She kicked her shoes off, then swung around on the arm of her chair and put her stockinged feet in my lap.

"My feet are cold," she said.

"It doesn't do to get cold feet at this stage of the game," I said.

She laughed and wiggled her toes.

"Feel that?" she asked.

"Yes."

She wiggled her toes some more.

Knuckles sounded on the door.

"Now what?" she asked.

"Your friends," I told her. "Here we go."

I put the champagne glass down, put my hands on her ankles, gently disengaged her feet, got up and walked to the door.

Two men in plain clothes stood there.

"Hello," I said.

One of the men pulled a leather folder out of his pocket, opened it, showed me a badge. "Police," he said. "We want to talk to you."

"Why, I . . . I—— What about?"

"We're coming in."

I stood barring the door.

"It wouldn't be convenient right at the moment," I said. "I will meet you in the lobby if you want."

One of the men stepped forward, his broad shoulder pushing me out of the way. "I said we're coming in," he announced. "Maybe you don't hear good."

I staggered back. The two men entered and closed the door.

I turned to look at Sharon.

She had her outer garments off and was standing there in bra, panties and stockings, holding a champagne glass in her hand and looking startled.

She was a long-stemmed, streamlined beauty, and she was really showing to advantage.

"Well, what in the world!" she exclaimed, and then said, "*Will* you men get out of here?"

"We want to talk with you," the spokesman said.

Sharon grabbed her clothes and shot into the bathroom.

One of the men walked over, picked up the bottle of champagne, smelled it, tested the temperature with his fingers, looked down in the carton, saw the other bottle of champagne and the glasses on dry ice and said, "Fancy party, huh?"

Sharon came out of the bathroom, pulling up the zipper on her dress.

"What is this all about?" she asked indignantly.

The officers seated themselves, one in the chair I had been sitting in, one on the bed.

The officer turned to me. "Your name Carleton Blewett?"

"No," I said.

He turned to Sharon. "Are you Mrs. Carleton Blewett?"

"No."

"Let's do a little checking. Let's see your driver's license."

"What is the meaning of this?" I asked.

"Well, right at the moment," the officer said, "we are checking to see whether you two rented sleeping quarters for immoral purposes."

"What are you talking about, immoral purposes?" I said. "We wanted to have a little champagne and you can't have that in the back seat of an automobile."

"So your girl friend took her clothes off, huh?"

I said, "She spilled some champagne on her dress when you folks pounded at the door and she wanted to wash it out before it left a stain."

"Yeah, I know. She was sitting here fully clothed when we knocked on the door," the officer said.

"That's right," I told him. "She was."

"All right, we'll check a few driving licenses. Let's see yours."

I took out my billfold and showed him my driving license. The officer wrote down the name and address. The other officer said to Sharon, "Okay, Sister, let's get yours out."

"This is an outrage," Sharon said.

"I know, I know. Let's get it over with. Let's take a look at the license."

She opened her purse, took out a wallet containing licenses and literally threw it at him.

He went through the whole thing, page by page.

He said to his brother officer, "This one is Sharon Barker, twenty-four, five feet seven, a hundred and fifteen pounds; evidently employed at the Cock and Thistle cocktail bar. I've got her social security number."

The other one said, "This fellow's name is Donald Lam —Hey, wait a minute! Aren't you a private detective?"

"That's right," I said.

"Well, I'll be damned," the officer said. "That makes it look a little different. My name's Smith. Suppose you start talking."

"What do you want me to talk about?"

"What you're doing here."

I said, "I came here with Sharon Barker for the purpose of having a little champagne party."

"And after that?"

I shrugged my shoulders and said, "Then I guess we'd have gone home. I didn't have a blueprint."

Someone rattled the door. One of the officers got up and opened it, and the man who came in was, I gathered, the security officer for the motel, which was more euphonious than the title of house detective. The officer said, "This is Donleavey Ralston, folks. He works here."

Ralston said, "That's the jane. I don't think this is the man."

"Don't you know?" the officer asked.

"No. He tried to keep his face turned but I saw his figure."

Smith turned to Sharon Barker. "What's your racket, Sister?" he asked.

"What do you mean, racket?"

"Come on, come on," Smith said. "We're trying to give you the breaks. Evidently you're doing a little high-class

prostitution. Do you want to go into the tank as a prostitute?"

"As a prostitute!" Sharon screamed. "Why, you——!"

"Take it easy," Smith interrupted. "We're giving you
the breaks, provided you talk."

"What do you want me to talk about?"

"You were here Saturday night. You registered as Mrs.
Carleton Blewett. You gave an address of two-five-four El
Belmont Drive, San Francisco. The people who are living
there never heard of a Carleton Blewett."

"That's a name I sort of made up."

"Why?"

"Why, I . . . I just somehow thought of it. I didn't
want to use real names. I made it all up out of thin air,
including the auto license number."

"All right," Smith said. "You're a big girl. If you're
collecting maybe a hundred dollars a night for this, you're
a prostitute."

"I'm collecting nothing. I don't charge money for my
. . . my friendship."

"You seem to have lots of friends."

"Is there anything wrong with that?"

"It depends on what you mean by wrong, and it
depends on how you define friendship. Now, let's do some
talking."

She said, "I'm a hostess at the Cock and Thistle. I try
to see that people who come there enjoy themselves and
get service. I get off around eleven every night and after
I'm off duty I'm on my own."

"All right, now tell us about Saturday."

"On Saturday, this man offered to take me to dinner.
He was lonely and I was footloose and we had dinner and
then we stopped to look at the lights of the city and . . ."

"Any necking?" the officer asked.

"Of course there was necking," she said indignantly.

"Do you think a man would sit looking at the lights with me without necking?"

"That's better," the officer said. "Then what happened?"

"Then he drove to this motel."

"When did he proposition you?"

"He didn't."

"Just drove right to the motel?"

"Yes."

"And you didn't raise a squawk when you saw what was happening?"

"I didn't raise a squawk," she said. "In case you want to know, I rather liked it. It was a novel approach. I don't like people that ask questions. It puts a girl in an embarrassing position, to have to say yes. And sometimes you don't feel like saying no. He just took things for granted and I rather liked it."

"You're doing better all the time," Smith said. "Keep talking."

"Well, that's about all there was to it. We got in here and had this same room and didn't have any baggage and my friend told the bellhop that he'd take the baggage out later. Then we sat around for a little while and he pulled out a pint of whiskey and we ordered setups and this gentleman who just came in brought them and we had a couple of drinks."

"And then what?"

"Then—well, I'm a champagne girl. I don't like whiskey, but after all we were here and . . . well, it helps sometimes to have a couple of drinks under your belt when you're . . . well, getting acquainted like that."

"Getting acquainted is good," Smith said. "Then what happened?"

"Well, the whiskey on top of the champagne didn't make me feel so good. I don't get exhilarated when I begin to get high on mixed drinks. I got a little dizzy and—I don't know. All of a sudden things started to go sour. My friend didn't look so good to me, and he was getting drunk."

"You went to bed?"

"I didn't go to bed."

"Oh, yeah?" Smith said.

"That's right!" she flared at him. "He started pawing and I got mad, walked out, called a taxi and went home. If you don't believe it, you can check with the taxi company and find that I ordered the taxi and got the hell out of here."

"About what time was that?" Smith asked, interested.

"About two o'clock in the morning."

"And what happened to the man?"

"I don't know what happened to him. I walked out on him. I never came back. He was just getting blotto when I left. I suppose he slept it off."

"What did he do?"

"There was only one thing for him to do. When he woke up, he got in his car and drove home."

"Where's home?"

"I don't know."

"How often had you seen him?"

"He'd been at the cocktail lounge once before."

Smith turned to me. "How did *you* get in on this act?"

"I met her this afternoon," I said. "We had a dinner date. I knew she liked champagne. I arranged with the restaurant to have some bottles on dry ice and some glasses. I thought I'd show my consideration for her tastes."

"And what did you expect to get out of it?"

"What do you think?"

Smith said, "All right. Now, I'll put it on the line. There was a murder here Saturday night or Sunday morning. The corpse was found Sunday morning. We're checking, and we're going to check on you two. If you're clean, you're not going to have any trouble. If you aren't, you're in for a hell of a lot of trouble. We can get the girl on suspicion of prostitution; we can throw the book at you. You know that."

I nodded.

"All right. Now, we want to know everything that happened Saturday night. Every little thing."

"I wasn't here," I said. "I'm not going to lie about it."

Smith turned to the girl. "We want to know everything you saw, everything you did, and we want to know who this man who was with you really is; that is, we want to know where we can put our finger on him."

She said, "We drove up at the office. There were two or three cars with people in them that were registering. Carleton, that's what he said I was to call him, didn't want to get out. He asked me to do the registering and to tell them at the desk that my husband and I had driven down from San Francisco and were tired.

"I dreamed up the San Francisco address, two-five-four El Belmont Drive. I went in and registered as Mr. and Mrs. Carleton Blewett of San Francisco and gave that address."

"What about the license number?"

"I just made up the name Blewett and a license number," she said.

"You've done this before?" Smith asked.

"What do you think?" she asked.

"For money?"

"No. I told you I don't give my friendship for money. I *work* for my money."

"Now, what time did you leave here and get a taxi? Remember, we can check up on that."

"I want you to check up on it. It was around . . . right around two o'clock in the morning, I think."

"You phoned for the cab?"

"Yes."

42

"From the office?"

"No."

"Where?"

"The phone booth."

"The phone booth out front?"

"Yes."

"Now, you had to walk right by the swimming pool to get to that phone booth."

"Not right by the swimming pool. The pool was fenced off by a railing. I went around the outside. The gate to the pool was closed."

"You're sure it was closed?"

"Yes."

"How do you know it was?"

"Because I wanted to cut through by the pool. It's shorter to go by the pool, but the near gate was closed."

"You're positive?"

"Positive."

"All right, you walked around on the outside of the railing. Now, the swimming pool was lighted."

"Yes."

"Could you see in it?"

"Not *down* in it, but the top of it."

"Was there water in it?"

"Yes. The pool was about half full. I remember seeing the reflections of the light in the water."

"Was anyone swimming in it, or anyone around it?"

"No."

"Could a body have been in it?"

"The way I was walking I couldn't see down into it. I could see the far side of the pool but I couldn't see all of it."

"But you didn't notice anything unusual?"

"No."

"Now look," Smith said, "in the morning when the body was found, the gate toward the telephone booth on the far side of the pool was open. The lock had been smashed."

"Well, the gate I passed was closed and locked when I went out. I can remember the gate was closed and I wondered if I could open it and I saw the chain and the padlock so then I went around the outside of the rail to the telephone booth and phoned for the cab."

"And what did you do while you were waiting for the cab?"

"Well, I just stood around and—just stood there."

"How long before the cab came?"

"About five minutes."

"Did you look in the pool while you were standing around there?"

"I don't remember. I don't think so."

"But the gates were both closed?"

"I think so."

"And locked?"

"I only know about the one gate toward the office. There was a chain and a padlock on it. I didn't see any chain on the other gate. I don't know if it was locked."

Smith's voice held a new note of friendliness. "Now look, Miss Barker," he said, "you've been a very great help to us. I want you to do some more thinking and see if you can remember anything else."

She narrowed her eyes, looked at the carpet for a moment, then slowly shook her head. "No," she said, "I can't remember anything else."

"The cab came?"

"Yes."

"Did you go out to the curb to meet the cab?"

"No. I was by the telephone booth, and the cabdriver got out and walked over to me."

"He asked if you were the one who had phoned for the cab?"

"Yes, he asked if I was Miss Barker and I told him I

44

was and—— Now, wait a minute, he said something about swimming."

"He did?" Smith asked, his voice showing excitement.

"That's right. He asked me if I had been swimming, or wanted to go swimming or something, and I said the water looked pretty cold, and he stood there beside me for a minute, looking at the water and then he said something about, 'Well, let's go.' "

"So then there was a cabdriver there at two o'clock in the morning who looked over at the pool?"

"Yes."

"And he was standing there with you near this telephone booth which was right by the back gate to the pool?"

"Yes."

Smith said, "This has been a *great* help to us, Miss Barker. I want to apologize for disturbing you. Now, what about this man, Carleton Blewett?"

"I don't know anything about him," she said, "except that he said I should call him Carleton. I made up the name of Blewett. I'd seen him once before in the cocktail lounge. And I know he couldn't tell you a thing. He had passed out. He was blotto."

"Is he married or single?"

"He never told me."

"Now look," Smith said, "you've been around. He didn't need to tell you. Was he married or single?"

"He was married," she said, "and I have an idea he hadn't done anything like this very often. He was a little embarrassed and I think he—well, I think he was a little ashamed and that's one of the things that made me mad.

"After all, if a man is going to do anything like that, he should make up his mind what he wants. He either wants it or he doesn't and—I don't know. He made me feel bad. He made me feel unclean somehow.

"After all, we're all human beings and we have human desires and human hungers and I'm no damned saint. On

45

the other hand I'm no hypocrite and I take life the way it comes. I liked him and I thought he liked me, and before we got here to the motel we were getting along swell.

"Up there on Mulholland Drive when we stopped, I liked him, and I liked the way he did it—just driving up to the motel. . . . All right, he'd made a sale as far as I was concerned.

"Then we got in here and he seemed to feel that he had to get drunk in order to go through with it, and to hell with it! I felt like slapping his face. I just wanted to get the hell out. As far as I'm concerned I never want to see him again and I guess he feels the same way about me, although he did ring up and want to know what the hell."

"And what did you tell him?"

"I told him what the hell."

"But you know the gate was closed when you went out; that is, the gate to the swimming pool."

"Yes."

"And he was here passed out," Smith said, "so he wouldn't be able to tell us anything."

"That's right."

Smith looked at the others. "Any more questions?"

They shook their heads.

Smith said, "Thanks, Miss Barker, for being a good scout—someday I'm going to drop in at the Cock and Thistle when I'm off duty. Perhaps I can buy you a dinner sometime."

"You're married," she said. "You told me I could tell, and I can tell."

He laughed and said, "Okay, Sister, you win. That's all, folks. We're sorry we disturbed the party. Go ahead, have fun."

The three men went out.

I turned to Sharon. "What was the idea?" I asked.

"Of what?"

"Taking your clothes off when I started for the door."

"I didn't take my clothes off," she said, "just my dress."

"All right, what was the idea taking your dress off?"

"It made it look more convincing. I wanted to take it off all along. I'd have done it sooner if you'd given me any encouragement, but you were so . . . so aloof, somehow, that it would have been . . . well, it would have been just cold turkey if I'd started undressing."

"All right," I said, "what do we do next?"

She said, "The man is supposed to take the initiative, isn't he?"

"In what way?"

"Oh, Donald, for heaven's sake, can't you give a girl some encouragement? I'm not going to do it *all*! "

"More champagne?" I asked.

"Yes," she snapped, "if that's what *you* want."

I tried the open bottle of champagne. It was still palatable but just a bit flat. She tossed off a glass in about three gulps and held it out for a refill.

I filled the glass and poured another quarter-inch in my own glass to fill it up.

I said, "Tell me, Sharon, did you really get a thousand dollars for this?"

"Uh-huh."

"Did that arouse your curiosity?"

"How do you mean?"

"Wasn't that rather steep?"

"What do you mean, steep?"

"I mean, isn't it a pretty high price for a little extra-curricular activity?"

"Now, wait a minute," she said, her eyes narrowing, "what do you mean by extracurricular activity? Do you mean what I think you mean?"

"No."

"Well, what *do* you mean?"

"I mean something that you picked up with a few hours' work that didn't interfere with your job."

"Look," she said, "a girl's good name is worth something."

"And who's going to hear about this except Inspector Smith?"

"Lots of people."

"Who?"

"The security officer here at the motel, for one."

"Would that make any difference?"

"Perhaps I might want to come here again."

"By yourself?"

"Don't be silly."

She held out her glass. When it was two-thirds full the bottle was finished. She looked at me thoughtfully. "Are you trying to wreck a perfectly good evening?"

"How?"

"All those questions."

"I was just trying to get the thing straight in my own mind."

"Do you have to have it straight?"

"I'd like to."

"All right, Donald," she said, "I'll tell you the truth and then we'll quit talking about it. I think the guy is some big-shot politician. He can't afford to be caught playing around. He doesn't dare give a statement to the police or let the police know who he is, therefore he had to work things so the police would leave him alone."

"You think they'll leave him alone now?"

"Sure they will. He was passed out and wasn't in a position to see anything. I'm the one that saw anything that was worth while."

"Such as what?"

"Such as the gate being closed at two o'clock in the morning."

"You think that's important?"

"The police did."

"You didn't seem to pay much attention to it until the police pointed out to you that it was important."

"I never gave it any thought. I was just hired to do a job and I did it."

"And you aren't going to try to find out who Carleton Blewett really is?"

"Why should I?"

"I thought perhaps you might have some curiosity."

"Well, I haven't. And I'll tell you something else, Donald Lam. If you know who he is, I don't want you to tell me."

"Why?"

"Well, information like that is dangerous. If I don't know I can't tell anybody, and that way I'd never have any temptation to shake the guy down. I mean I wouldn't be in a position to, even if I wanted to. And that will help."

"How do you mean?"

"In my line of work a girl can get to know too much."

"They say knowledge is power," I said.

"Sometimes it leads to corpses in motel rooms. I don't want to be found with one of my nylon stockings wrapped around my neck. . . . Donald, how much are *you* getting out of this?"

"Not half enough," I told her.

"That doesn't answer my question. I told you what I was getting."

"And I told you I wasn't getting half enough. I don't like this."

"Why not?"

"There may be some repercussions."

"Oh, bosh!" she said. "You're out of the woods. It went through just like clockwork. Tell me, Donald, did I put on a good act?"

"What acting did you do?"

"Grabbing my dress and holding it in front of me, backing toward the bathroom and then suddenly turning

49

when I closed the door. I'll bet those officers got a good view."

"They see lots of good views."

"I'll bet you got a good view."

"I did."

"You don't seem very excited about it."

"Right now I've got other things to think of."

"Such as what?"

"Inspector Smith."

"What about him?"

"How did you size him up?"

"A good Joe. He was just a little on the make, too. Did you notice the way he threw out a line about coming down to the Cock and Thistle sometime?"

"Uh-huh."

"And I came right back and told him he was married."

"Does that stop them?" I asked.

"It stops me," she said.

She was silent for a moment or two, then she said, "Why did you ask about Inspector Smith, Donald?"

"Because," I said, "if he wanted to play dirty or if he felt that you hadn't been giving him one hundred per cent co-operation, he could put us in a hell of a spot."

"How come?"

"That rooming-house ordinance," I said. "And if he should throw you in on a charge of lewd conduct . . ."

"Why did you stop talking, Donald?"

"I was just thinking."

"Dammit! " she said. "You do too much thinking. You use your head when you should be using your hands."

We sat silent for a few moments.

Abruptly she got to her feet, ran her hands up her stockings, looked in the mirror. "Know something, Donald?"

"What?"

"I've got news for you."

"What?"

"I'm going home."

"Ill take you."

"No, you won't. I'm going in a cab."

I opened my wallet. "I'll give you cab money."

"You're not making any attempt to hold me here."

"Is that what you want?"

"Dammit, Donald, you're not very flattering to a woman. You make me feel like a warmed-over dish of cat meat. To hell with you."

She threw her coat around her, picked up her purse, said, "Good night and good-by."

I watched her walk out.

CHAPTER 5

I WAITED five minutes, then put the key in my pocket, went out, closed the door behind me, walked down past the swimming pool to the phone booth at the end of the walk.

The front gate at the swimming pool was closed and padlocked. The back gate had a spring lock. It was closed.

I eased into the telephone booth, dropped a dime and dialed the number of Elsie Brand.

The phone rang repeatedly and then I heard Elsie's voice.

She was good and angry. "Hello!" she snapped. "And who's ringing at this hour?"

"Donald," I said.

"Donald!" she exclaimed, and suddenly her voice softened. "What it is, Donald? Are you in trouble?"

"I need some help."

"Donald, tell me where you are. I'll do anything I can. I'll come to you. What can I do?"

I said, "Drive by the office, go to my desk, pick up my fingerprint-dusting outfit and a roll of lifting tape. Then drive to the Bide-a-wee-bit Motel. I'm in Unit 27. Now, don't drive your car into the parking place or past the office of the motel. There's a swimming pool at the northeast corner and there's a telephone booth by the swimming pool at the far end. You can get to the booth from the sidewalk. Park your car at the curb at that point. Go to the telephone booth and go through the motions of making calls until you see the coast is clear. Then leave the place and walk directly to Unit 27.

"Unit 27 is the third one from the end on the next-to-the-last row of units. In other words, when you come from the swimming pool you'll walk along the fence and you'll see six rows of cabins on your left and then a parking space and over on the other side of the parking place there are eight or ten rows of cabins.

"You keep to the left. Go to the second tier from the end, turn left and Unit 27 is the third one from the end. Walk right in. I'll have the door unlocked."

"Donald, are you . . . alone?"

"Yes."

"Donald, it'll take me a little while to dress and get to the office. It'll be . . . it'll be forty-five minutes or perhaps an hour before I can get there."

"It's all right," I told her. "Take your time."

I hung up the phone, walked back to Unit 27, fixed the latch on the door so it would remain open, stretched out on top of one of the beds, punched the pillows under my head and lay there thinking.

After a while I began to doze off, then sank into a sound sleep, despite the fact I was determined to keep awake.

I dreamed that soft feminine lips were pressed gently against mine. I could smell the haunting aroma of sweet flowers.

Then suddenly I wakened. Elsie Brand was standing by the bed, looking down at me with a peculiar expression on her face.

"Donald," she said, "I wakened you, didn't I?"

"I wanted you to waken me. We have work to do."

She stood looking down at me. "You were smiling Donald," she said. "Smiling in your sleep. Were you dreaming?"

"Yes."

"Was it a nice dream, Donald?"

"Very nice."

"What was it?"

"You'd slap my face."

"Donald! What was it, Donald?"

"I dreamed I was holding you in my arms and kissing you."

"Donald!" she exclaimed. "You mustn't say things like that. You . . ."

"I told you you'd get mad but you asked me."

"Donald, were you *really* dreaming that?"

"Yes."

I struggled up to a sitting position, shook my head, ran my fingers through my hair, and said, "You brought all the stuff?"

"Yes. . . . Donald, you're tired. You're working too hard."

I said, "We can finish up here in a couple of hours. Then I'll try and get some sleep."

"What happened, Donald? What happened to the . . . the girl?"

"She got mad and went home."

'Why did she get mad, because you . . . because you . . . ?"

"No," I said, "because I didn't."

She suddenly laughed and said, "It serves her just good and right, taking you for granted. . . . What do we do?"

"I'm going to go over this place for fingerprints," I said. "You're going to come along behind me and clean and polish everything I touch so that no one knows the surfaces have been dusted."

"What are you looking for, Donald?"

"Fingerprints."

"Whose fingerprints?"

"Anyone who touched anything."

"That girl?"

"Hers."

"Who else?"

"I don't know."

"All right, Stingy," she said, "don't tell me if you don't want to."

"I've told you," I said. "I don't know."

I went to the bathroom, closed the door, took a Kleenex from the box, rubbed it over my mouth. It came away with the faint pink of lipstick on it.

I tasted my lips and got just the faintest flavor of raspberry.

I dropped the Kleenex down the toilet, came back out and said, "Let's go to work."

I started in with the telephone. Then I went to the metal headboards and supports for the beds. I tried the underside of the dressing table and the edge of the adjustable oval mirror. I dusted around the medicine cabinet in the bathroom, the toothbrush holder, the frames of the windows, the under edges of the chairs and table top.

From time to time I developed good fingerprints. When I did, I'd put lifting tape on them, number the print, dictate to Elsie the place where the print came from, and put the lift in the container on my fingerprint outfit.

Then Elsie would take a washrag, soap and water, and clean the place where I'd dusted so that no one could tell the surface had been tested for latents.

By three o'clock in the morning I had fifteen good, legible fingerprints; without, of course, having the faintest idea who had made them.

"Now what?" Elsie asked, when we had finished.

"Now," I said, "we go and have some ham and eggs."

"What's this corrugated cardboard package?"

"That," I said, "is champagne, champagne glasses and dry ice."

"Donald, you lifted a print from one of these champagne glasses—the one with lipstick on it."

"That's right."

"And I washed it. Was that all right?"

"That's all right," I said. "Wash them and put them in the container."

"I didn't know they fitted into the container. I had just put them over here on the dresser."

"All right," I said, "we'll put them in the container."

"Now what do we do?"

I said, "You go to your car, I'll go to mine. You follow me. I'll drive slow and keep watching the rearview mirror."

"Where do we go?"

"To a restaurant."

"Donald, can't you get . . . a couple of hours' sleep?"

"It's an idea," I said. "What would you do?"

"I'd . . . I'd wait in the car."

"Don't be silly."

"All right, I'd . . . I'll—— What do you want, Donald?"

I moved over to one side of the bed. "Put your head down on my arm and we can both get an hour or so and that'll help. Then we can go get breakfast."

"Donald, I . . . I couldn't."

"Why couldn't you?"

I pulled my coat tightly around me and stretched my arm out on the pillow.

She hesitated a moment, then gently slid over on the edge of the bed and put her head on my arm. After a few moments she relaxed, and I moved over against the warmth of her body.

Five minutes later I was asleep.

When I wakened it was daylight and she was cuddled up against me.

I raised on one elbow, looking down at her.

Her lips quivered slightly, then her eyes fluttered open.

For a moment she couldn't place herself and was startled as she saw me looking down at her. Then she said, "Donald, what—— What . . ."

"Time to get up," I told her.

56

"Oh," she said, but made no immediate move toward getting up.

I said, "We're going to have to get breakfast and get to work."

She raised her hands, rubbed gentle finger tips over my face.

"And you're going to get a shave."

"Think I'd scratch?" I asked.

"I . . . I wouldn't mind," she said, and then suddenly her arms were around me and she pulled me down close to her.

We lay there for another five or ten minutes. Then suddenly she pushed me away and jumped to her feet, shaking her skirt down.

"Donald," she said, "what must you think of me?"

"Why?"

"Doing things like that."

"That's necking," I said. "Haven't you ever necked?"

"In an automobile but not . . . not . . ."

"Does the place make any difference?" I asked.

"Yes," she said, her face flaming. She dashed into the bathroom and slammed the door.

I got up and ran a pocket comb through my hair. Ten minutes later, when she was out, I went in, washed my face in cold water and then said, "Remember to follow me, Elsie. And if anybody should cut in between us, you just turn your car at the first corner and beat it for home."

"Why? What would it mean if anybody did cut in between us?"

"It would mean someone was following me. Now, you leave here first. Go out and get in your car and get the motor warmed up. Then watch the exit which is right around to the left of where you have your car parked. When I come out, follow me."

I gave her a good head start, then walked out, got in my

car, started the motor and after it had warmed up a bit, drove leisurely out of the parking place.

Elsie came tagging along behind and no one tried to get in between us.

I drove to an intimate little restaurant which I knew and we had breakfast.

"All right," I told her, "you go home, and then come to the office in the regular way. I'll be in after a while."

"Donald, you won't . . . won't think I'm forward, will you?"

I patted her shoulder. "You're a sweet kid, Elsie."

"Donald, I—— It was nice . . . and *you're* nice."

I escorted her over to her automobile, opened the door for her. She got in. I watched her legs. She self-consciously pulled her skirt down with a nervous little laugh. "Donald," she said, "you're staring."

"Is that against the law?"

"It's . . . it's embarrassing."

"They're nice," I said.

She slammed the car door, stepped on the starter and drove away fast.

I got in my car, drove to my apartment, took out all the finger lifts, studied them with a magnifying glass, trying to familiarize myself with the different patterns. Then I put the fingerprints in a package, addressed the package to myself at the swanky Edgemount Motel, sealed it, drove to a branch post office and sent it special delivery.

CHAPTER 6

BERTHA COOL was beaming all over her face.

"Congratulations, Partner," she said.

"On what?" I asked.

"On bringing the job to a successful completion, of course."

"It isn't completed, and it wasn't successful," I told her.

Her face fell. "What in hell are you talking about?"

I said, "That kind of a job doesn't get washed up that easy."

"Nonsense," she said. "Everything went off like clockwork."

"How do you know?"

"Our client telephoned."

"How did he know?"

"Sharon Barker told him."

"And how did Sharon Barker know where she could communicate with him?"

Bertha thought that over for a few seconds, then said, "That's right, I guess she didn't. He must have called her."

"Pretty early in the morning to be calling a hostess in a cocktail lounge," I said. "Most girls who work until almost midnight, then go out to dinner and then spend the night in a motel, would resent being called before nine o'clock in the morning."

"Oh, don't be such a damned skeptic!" Bertha said. "After all, the guy told me he'd paid her a thousand dollars, and when you're giving a cocktail hostess a grand you can call her at any hour of the morning."

59

"What did he say?" I asked.

"He said that everything went like clockwork, that he would be up here within an hour to give us a little bonus. He said it would have been more if he hadn't had to give the girl a grand. That certainly is making money the easy way—for you, I mean!"

"Easy?"

"My God, yes!" Bertha stormed. "You take some good-looking doll up to a motel, spend the night with her and we get paid two thousand smackers for it. What the hell more do you want? I take it she was good-looking?"

"Beautiful," I said.

"Figure?"

"Streamlined, long-legged; curves but not bulges; beautiful eyes."

"Aren't you the lucky bastard."

"Am I?"

"You know damned well you are."

"No, I don't. This is a murder case, Bertha."

"So what?"

"Don't underestimate the police."

"Phooey! We haven't done anything wrong."

I said, "I'm telling you—don't underestimate the police."

"All right then, I won't underestimate the police. So what does that mean?"

"Your friend, Frank Sellers," I said, "is . . ."

"Here now," Sellers said, from the doorway.

Bertha looked up and said, "How the hell did you get in without being announced?"

"I told the switchboard operator not to ring," Sellers said.

"Well, you've got a crust! That switchboard operator happens to be taking orders from me!"

"This time she took them from me."

Sellers stood in the doorway, grinning; a great big hulk of broad-shouldered, competent cop, enjoying Bertha's discomfiture.

"Well, what do you want?" Bertha asked.

"What I want," Sergeant Sellers said, "is the low-down."

"On what?"

"On the caper Donald cut last night."

"What kind of a caper?"

"You know what kind of a caper. Don't play dumb."

"Well, ask Donald," she said. "My God, has this town got so damned puritanical a fellow can't pick up a good-looking babe and take her to a motel without calling in the whole damned police force?"

"It has been done," Sellers said. "Doubtless it is being done, and it probably will be done again. But in this particular instance, while we haven't brought in the whole police force, I've been brought in, and I'm curious."

Sellers walked over to a chair, settled himself, pulled a cigar out of his pocket, thrust it in the side of his mouth, but didn't light it. He looked from me to Bertha, then back to me.

"Okay," he said, "spill it."

I said, "I took this dame to a motel. It happened she'd been there Saturday night with another boy friend. He'd paid for two or three days. Guess he thought it would be a long party. It also happened that Saturday night was the night Ronley Fisher was found murdered right in the swimming pool of that same motel."

"What happened last night?" Sellers asked.

"My sleep was interrupted," I said.

"Too bad," Sellers said. "I understand the boys went away afterwards and left you to your own devices."

"Did they?" I asked.

"Well, almost."

"What do you mean, almost?" Bertha asked.

Sellers turned to her, chewed the cigar over to the other side of his mouth and said, "The boys were a little curious. You can't blame them for that. The taxpayers pay us for being curious. So we put a stake-out on the motel to see how Donald's love affair was progressing. Evidently it didn't progress."

"How come?" Bertha asked.

"The girl walked out on him within half an hour, telephoned for a taxi, and went home. It seems to be a habit she has."

Bertha looked at me, her eyes snapping.

"Then," Sellers said, "Donald went out and looked around; then went and telephoned and was joined by another dame."

"Another dame!" Bertha screamed.

"That's right," Sellers said.

"Well, fry me for an oyster!" Bertha exclaimed.

Sellers said, "Now, here's the way we dope it out. Donald wasn't there with this Sharon Baker on a date, he was there on business. After the business was concluded, he got rid of Sharon and sent for the girl he really wanted to have a date with.

"Donald was playing it pretty cozy. The motel was all paid for, the expected interruptions which he had been waiting for were all over, and there was no reason why Donald couldn't have himself a nice little time."

"Who was this babe? Do you know?" Bertha asked.

"Of course we know," Sellers said. "We made it our business to find out. She's Donald's secretary."

"Well, I'll . . . be . . . damned!" Bertha said.

"Surprised?" Sellers asked.

"Hell, no," Bertha said. "Not in a way—I didn't know it had gone that far, that's all. That secretary of his is moon-eyed every time she looks at him, but I didn't know they were playing footsies. It looked more like a case of frustration to me. My God, she blushes every time Donald looks at her and . . ." She turned to me. "So you finished up the night with her, eh?"

I didn't say anything.

After a while Bertha said, "Well, so what? I guess they're both old enough to know what they're doing."

"You don't get the sketch," Sellers said.

"The hell I don't!" Bertha snapped.

"You don't, at that," Sellers said. "The fact that Donald finished up the evening with the girl of his choice simply confirms our idea that Donald's activities during the first part of the evening were purely professional. Now then, we want to know the name of your client."

Bertha simply glared at him.

"Sharon Barker is a pretty nice babe," Sellers said. "As far as we know she isn't selling anything. She's inclined to be generous at times and that's okay with us. If she wants to play it that way, it's her business.

"However, she doesn't have the kind of money that would pay a detective to go out and set up a plant with her, and that makes us more curious about the identity of your real client."

"Perhaps she didn't pay in money," Bertha said.

"We considered that possibility," Sellers said, "and wiped it out. As long as you're a partner in this detective agency, it was a money deal. Now then, who was your client?"

Bertha shook her head. "You know we can't do that."

"This is a murder case," Sellers said, "and we're not beating around the bush. Who was your client?"

Bertha looked at me.

I shook my head.

Sellers said, "No word of this is going to leak out on the outside, but we want to know."

I said, "That's one thing we can't tell you."

Sellers' face darkened. He clamped his jaw until the cigar was pushed upward at a truculent angle. "This is once I'm not going to take no for an answer, Pint Size," he said.

Bertha said, "Look, Frank, it's on the up and up. This man was a married man. He's in a ticklish position. He has his good name to protect."

"We'll protect his good name," Sellers said. "We'll protect him all the way down the line, but we want to know. We want to check, and we want to talk with him. You can collect another fee for working out a deal with us by which he'll be protected."

Again Bertha glanced at me.

I said, "We can't do it, Sellers. This man could have our license if we did."

"And I'll damned well have your license if you don't," Sellers snapped.

"You can't get it on those grounds."

"Maybe I can and maybe I can't, but I'll get it on some grounds. You aren't going to play cozy with us in a murder case of this importance."

Bertha said, "The man came to us for protection. He's paying us——"

"Shut up, Bertha," I said.

Bertha glared at me.

Sellers got to his feet.

"Okay," he said, "if I can't get it the easy way, I'll get it the hard way. I'll get it, and after I get it I'll remember what happened and how it happened."

Bertha said, "Maybe we can get his permission to give you his name if you'll promise to protect him."

"I'll promise to protect him, provided his nose is clean," Sellers said. "Otherwise, I'll throw him to the wolves."

Bertha said, "Give us a ring in an hour, Frank."

Frank Sellers paused with his hand on the doorknob. His eyes narrowed thoughtfully. Abruptly he said, "All right," and walked out.

I waited until he was far enough away from the door to

be out of earshot, then said to Bertha in a low voice, "Get Carleton Allen on the phone."

"There's no need to. He's on his way in here."

"That's it," I told her. "You've got to head him off."

"Why?"

I said, "You let the cat out of the bag. You told Sellers to get in touch with you in an hour. That means that he knows you're going to be in touch with your client. He knows that you'd hardly want to present a matter of this delicacy over the telephone. Sellers is going to have the office shadowed. Get hold of Allen and tell him not to come in."

"I can't do it," Bertha said. "He's on his way up here right now."

"All right," I said. "I'm going down and wait in the lobby. When Allen walks in the building I'm going to stick a note in his hand and tell him to go to one of the other offices, but not to come to this office."

"If Sellers catches you doing that he'll raise hell," Bertha said.

"Let him raise hell," I told her. "It's up to us to protect our client."

I grabbed a piece of paper and scrawled a note: "Police have our office under surveillance. Go to the elevator, go to the floor above ours. There's an income tax expert on that floor. Go in and ask him some questions. Don't go near our offices until we give you the word. Call up later on and find out if the coast is clear."

I left the office, took the elevator to the lobby and went to the cigar counter.

I'd heard the blonde who ran the cigar counter was on the make. Fifty bucks a night and transportation both ways would get her anyplace any time.

That being so, I felt she'd like to discuss matters.

It turned out that was right.

I bought cigarettes and acted a little on the make. I

moved to the end of the counter. She'd come down to talk to me between customers.

Carleton Allen walked in when she was getting ready to close a deal. He was looking at the elevators and didn't see me. I brushed against him, shoved the note into his hand, said, "Pardon me," and was out of the building before his reaction time had set in.

I didn't *think* anyone was watching.

I hoped the stake-out would be on the floor where we had our offices. Sellers couldn't have got enough men to sew up the whole building in the short time in which he'd had to work.

CHAPTER 7

THE address which Carleton Allen had given us on his business card did not tell the whole story.

The card had simply been *Carleton Allen, President, Allen Enterprises,* with an office address.

The address, however, turned out to be that of the *Getchell & Allen Investment Management Corporation,* and the Allen Enterprises was merely one of the half-dozen subsidiary companies which were listed.

Tucking the brief case which contained my fingerprinting outfit under my arm, I told the receptionist that I wanted to talk to Mr. Allen's private secretary upon a matter of the greatest importance. It was, I assured her, a matter which I could only disclose to Mr. Allen's personal secretary.

After a bit of telephone conversation I was passed through a door, sent down a long corridor, and into a richly carpeted office where an exceptionally good-looking young woman, radiating efficiency, presided at a desk.

Behind this desk were two doors, one bearing the legend, *Carleton Allen,* and the other the words, *Marvin Getchell.*

The office had several deeply cushioned chairs, but fortunately those chairs were unoccupied at the moment.

I advanced to the desk, holding my brief case clamped tightly under my arm.

"You're Mr. Allen's private secretary?" I asked.

"Yes," she said. "I am Miss Beal. I believe you have a confidential matter to discuss?"

"That's right," I said, and produced one of my cards.

"I'm Donald Lam of Cool and Lam. Does that mean anything to you?"

Her eyes narrowed. "You're Mr. Lam?"

"Yes."

"Do you have any identification with you, Mr. Lam?"

I produced my driving license.

She checked it carefully, said, "Very well. What was the nature of the information you wish me to transmit to Mr. Allen?"

"I want to see him," I said. "As you may know, he left our offices not too long ago. Unfortunately, circumstances existed which prevented me telling him something of very considerable importance and I want to get word to him right away. How soon do you expect him in?"

"He telephoned that he would be here within half an hour. That was about five minutes ago."

I frowned. "Hang it! I've *got* to see him."

"Would you care to wait, Mr. Lam?"

I looked around the office and shook my head. "Not here," I said. "I don't want anyone to see me, particularly someone who may be coming in *here*. . . . I'll tell you what I'll do; I'll wait as long as I can in his private office. As soon as he comes in, call him over and tell him I'm in there but be careful that anyone else who may be in the office doesn't hear my name or know that I'm waiting inside."

I needed all of my assurance as I moved past her desk and calmly opened the door of Allen's private office.

I didn't dare go too fast, I didn't dare go too slow. I didn't dare create the impression that I needed her permission. I had to adopt the attitude of a man who is sufficiently close to her boss so he knows that anything he wants to do will be all right.

For a fraction of a second she seemed hesitant. Then she accepted the situation, somewhat dubiously, but nevertheless she accepted it.

I closed the door of Allen's private office behind me.

It was an office fitted for utility. The steel desk, with a heavy composition top, contained drawers subdivided into compartments for holding cards, letter files and legal documents.

The chairs were modernistic but comfortable. A bookcase contained a couple of dozen reference books.

I waited just long enough to make sure the secretary was not going to follow me into the office, then moved over to the desk.

I took dusting powder from my brief case and went over the polished metal ornamental rim around the side of the desk.

A couple of dozen latent fingerprints came to life. Six or eight of them were smudged but the balance were good enough to be lifted.

I placed lifting tape over the prints, hurriedly lifted them, then took a chamois skin from my brief case and polished the desk.

I stepped to the door and opened it a crack.

"Miss Beal," I said, "will you look in here, please?"

She jumped up from her chair as though my words had triggered an electric current.

I stepped back as she opened the door and entered the office.

"Is anyone out there in the outer office?" I asked.

She shook her head.

I said, "I was hoping I could wait until Mr. Allen came in, but I'm not going to be able to make it. I have a very important message I want you to deliver to him."

"Yes," she said.

I said, "Tell him that under no circumstances is he to have any contact with the young woman I saw last night."

"The young woman you saw last night?"

"Yes."

"Could you give me her name?"

I shook my head. "Just remember that—the young woman I saw last night."

"Will he know whom you mean?"

"He'll know," I said.

"Very well," she said. "I'll tell him."

"Remember," I said, "under *no* circumstances is he to see her."

"I understand, and I shall tell him that you left that message."

"If you will, please. Now look out in the outer office. If the coast is clear, signal me and I'll leave. If it isn't, get rid of the person who is there and let me know as soon as it's clear."

She opened the door, looked out, turned and said, "Okay, Mr. Lam."

I went out, the brief case under my arm.

I flashed her one quick glance as I left the outer office, giving her a reassuring smile.

She didn't smile back. Her eyes were clouded with doubt and were focused on the brief case under my arm.

CHAPTER 8

I MADE certain no one was following me and drove to the Edgemount Motel. I registered under my own name and asked for mail. They gave me the special delivery package. I hung a "Do not disturb" sign on the door, spread out the lifted fingerprints and went to work.

I couldn't be certain about the fingerprints that had been lifted from the room in the motel, except those Sharon had left on the champagne glass. They might have been fingerprints from chambermaids, from previous occupants or from visitors. I couldn't be certain of the fingerprints I had lifted from the highly polished metal rim around the desk in Allen's private office. Some were undoubtedly his, some probably belonged to his secretary, some could have been from business visitors who had called upon him in connection with his various business activities.

What I really wanted at the moment was to find whether *one* of the latents I had lifted from the desk in Allen's private office would coincide with *one* of the fingerprints I had lifted from the room in the motel.

Half an hour after I started to work I made my match.

There could be no doubt of it. One of the fingerprints I had lifted from the desk of Allen's private office coincided with a fingerprint I had lifted from the motel unit.

I thought things over for five minutes, then called our office and asked the operator to put Bertha Cool on the line.

"Where the hell are *you*?" Bertha rasped at me.

"Working," I said.

"Well, the phone's been ringing and people have been wanting you."

"Let them want," I told her. "I just wanted you to know that I'm going to be out of circulation for a while."

"What do you mean, a while?"

"Until the heat's off."

"What heat?"

"You'll find out."

"There isn't any heat."

"Then keep cool," I told her, and hung up.

I had contacts I could depend on for registration information. I got busy on the phone tracing the ownership of the car having license number VGH 535.

The car turned out to be a Cadillac owned by Carlotta Shelton.

Carlotta Shelton was big time, a long-legged divorcee with a background of yachts, horses and golf—a member of the country club set.

So if Sharon was telling the truth, Carlotta's car had been parked at the motel on Saturday night.

But was she telling the truth? Carlotta's name had never been mentioned in connection with the case, either by the press or, so far as I could learn, by the police.

Yet if her name entered the case, it would be news.

If she had been at that motel Saturday night, she had been registered under another name—and why would a divorcee with a big, fat alimony check coming in every month, a swank apartment of her own, have been at the Bide-a-wee-bit Motel?

Or had Sharon been lying?

Sharon had used a license number on which she had changed just one letter. She could hardly have just dreamed up that license number and then had it fit on the late model Cadillac to which it rightfully belonged.

I decided to give that situation just a hell of a lot more thought.

CHAPTER 9

THE coroner had been having some arguments with the chief of police. People who didn't like the guy had been trying to get him on the defensive. One of his deputies, James C. Lowden, handled public relations for the office and was inclined to be obliging wherever possible. I knew him by sight.

It took me an hour before I got in to see him.

He looked at my official card and said, "What can I do for you, Lam?"

I said, "Insurance companies are a nuisance, aren't they?"

He started to nod, then the old public relations instinct came to the foreground and he said, "Well, of course, Lam, you can't blame them. They have to be sure."

"I know," I said, "but sometimes they seem to spend lots of time and money chasing themselves around in circles."

"And," he said, smiling, "I suppose you are representing an insurance company, are preparing to cause us a lot of trouble, and this is your way of breaking the ice."

"Could be," I told him. "What about Ronley Fisher?"

His face turned to wood. "What about him, Lam?"

"Autopsy show anything?"

"Look, Lam, that's a police murder case. You know I can't say anything about that."

"I don't mean about who murdered the guy," I said. "I mean from an insurance angle."

"What do you mean, from an insurance angle?"

"Any question about the identification?"

"Good heavens, no."

"Any question about it being suicide?"

"You tell me how a man can cave in the back of his own head and then we'll talk over suicide. The way this blow was struck it would have been just about a physical impossibility for Fisher to have inflicted the wound himself. Moreover, when people want to commit suicide they don't club themselves to death. They take poison, jump into a lake, shoot themselves or take an overdose of sleeping pills. They don't take a baseball bat and swing it down on top of their heads."

I said, "Look, Lowden, I'm just trying to make a living. Suppose there hadn't been any water in that swimming pool and Fisher had thought there had been. Fisher goes over to the springboard, comes up in the air and takes a high dive. He comes down expecting to hit the water and nine feet later he hits a slab of concrete."

Lowden said, "After all, Lam, that's something I can't talk about. You know that."

"It would interest the insurance company."

"Then the insurance company will have to dig up the evidence."

"All right," I told him, "let's just check on the question of identity."

"What are you talking about—identity?" Lowden said. "Good lord, the guy is well known all over town."

"I know, I know," I said, "but you know how insurance companies are."

"What company you working for?" Lowden asked.

"I didn't say," I told him. "I didn't even say I was working for an insurance company. All I said was that I was trying to get this thing cleaned up and of course insurance companies have a procedure that's pretty well standardized in cases of this sort. Naturally I'm trying to keep my investigative work up to the standard of insurance specifications."

He laughed and said, "Which is a lot of double talk for

telling me that you have already been retained by the insurance company and they don't want anyone to know that they're making an investigation on the Q.T."

"And the investigation checks as to identification?"

"Of course it does. Good lord, Lam, what are you getting at? Do you know something?"

"I don't know anything. I'm just trying to get the details all checked. What about fingerprints? You take his fingerprints?"

"Of course we took his fingerprints. We take the fingerprints of everyone that goes through here."

"Check them with the government files of his fingerprints?"

"Hell, no," Lowden said. "That is, not yet. We didn't have any intention of making the check until you came along and started talking about identification."

"You have his prints?"

"I told you, yes."

"Can I take a look at the file?"

"No."

"At his prints?"

Lowden hesitated for a moment, then said, 'Sure, why not? I'll get you the prints."

He went out of the office into a filing room and came back with a set of ten prints.

"How about pulling me a copy?"

He hesitated a moment, then said, "Why not?" went over to a duplicating machine and made a copy of the prints.

"That do it all right?" he asked.

"I think so," I told him. "That copy is plain enough for purposes of comparison."

"Lam, what's the idea on his identity?"

"How would I know? All I know is that I want to double check the identification so there can't be any question about *that* phase of the case."

"Someone has asked you the question?"

"That," I said, "is hard to say."

"You mean it's hard for *you* to say."

"Have it your own way." I laughed.

"All right, Lam, you've got the fingerprints and I'm making a note that the insurance company may be raising a question as to identification."

"Don't do that," I said.

"Why?"

"Because it won't be true."

"Well, what is true?"

"About all you can say is really established in this case is that the victim was Ronley Fisher. He was the trial deputy in charge of the murder trial of Staunton Cliffs, who is being tried for the murder of his wife. It's a case that has attracted a lot of attention. Therefore Fisher was very much in the public eye and his murder has caused a lot of people to ask a lot of questions.

"That much," I told him, "you have for certain. Anything over and beyond that, you're guessing at."

"Any harm in guessing?" he asked.

"Not if you come up with the right answers."

"And suppose I should come up with the wrong answers?"

I held my eyes on him. "That would be bad for you," I said, "and bad for the office."

"Now, wait a minute, Lam. The office has had enough trouble. Let's not make any more."

"That's the way I felt about it," I told him.

"All right, let's put it this way: If an insurance company is working on any angle that might pan out, it would help a lot if we could know what the angle was."

"So you could tell the police?"

"That would help."

"Would it?"

"Sure, it would. The police have been—well, not as co-operative as they could be."

"So you'd come to them with some new angle on a case and the police would think that perhaps at some time in the future the office would use it to make itself look good and make the police look bad," I said. "That would be nice, wouldn't it?"

He grinned, a wry grin, and said, "Come to think of it, that would not be nice."

"In other words," I said, "when you come to think of it, you're getting along fine just the way you are."

"Just so you don't come up with anything that would make *us* look bad."

I said, "I've simply asked you what you're doing about checking identification and whether there was any possibility there was an erroneous identification."

"And what did I tell you?"

"You told me that all you knew about the case was what your findings disclosed and that you weren't in a position to tell me anything about what that was."

"And I let you look at the file?"

"No. You gave me a set of fingerprints from the file so that I could check the man's identity in case there was any mistake about it."

"All right," he said, "suppose there should be some mistake in the—well, in the fingerprints?"

"How could there be?"

"Perhaps—hell, I don't know, Lam, but stranger things have happened. It might be that Ronley Fisher was killed in the war and somebody picked up his dog tags and identification and came back and started living his life from there on."

I said, "You've been watching too many television shows. But you have his fingerprints and the government would have his fingerprints, so if you want to be sure

77

everything's okay, why don't you just check with the FBI on fingerprints?"

"If you think we won't do it, you're crazy," he said. "Now that you've acted so inquisitive and so damned mysterious about it, we'll even check his footprint in the hospital where he was born.

"Now, get the hell out of here so I can close up the office and go home."

I left the place, went back to the motel and started checking fingerprints.

All of a sudden I came bolt upright in my chair. I had another match. One of Ronley Fisher's fingerprints matched one of the latents I had developed and lifted from Unit 27 in the Bide-a-wee-bit Motel.

Now the agency was mixed in a murder case up to its eyebrows.

For a private detective to be in possession of that sort of information was like standing on the brink of the crater of a volcano which was just about to erupt, or wandering around in a dark powder magazine and striking matches to find out where the door was.

The big trouble was that fingerprints carry no time label.

If the murdered man had been in the room with Sharon Barker and Carleton Allen, I had to play it one way, and in only one way.

But suppose Ronley Fisher had been there *before* they arrived?

Some motels make a habit of renting accommodations several times in one night.

This motel wasn't in that category, or shouldn't have been, but many a façade of respectability has hidden all sorts of irregularities.

How could I be certain about the aura of respectability which clung to this motel?

In the event that unit had been rented twice, it was only

natural for the management to suppress the records of the first rental. In that event the management of the motel was in just as much of a predicament as I was.

I went to a phone booth, got the number of Carlotta Shelton's apartment, dialed the number and said to the woman who answered the telephone, "Is Mrs. Shelton there, please?"

"Who shall I say is calling?"

"A man who has some very important information about Saturday night," I said.

"Your name, please?"

"Mr. Knight."

"And the first name?"

"Saturday."

"I'm afraid I can't approach Mrs. Shelton with a message of that sort. Mr. Saturday Knight, you say?"

"That's right," I told her. "Knight. K-n-i-g-h-t."

"Yes, I got that, but the other name."

"The first name," I said, "is Saturday."

"Saturday Knight?" the voice said. "I am afraid . . .".

I heard a woman's voice. "Rosa, what in the world *are* you talking about?"

There was a moment of silence. Rosa evidently had put her palm over the mouthpiece of the telephone while she explained to Carlotta Shelton.

A moment later the voice of another woman came over the line, a voice that was guarded, cautious and cold.

"Could you tell me more about your business, Mr. Knight?"

I took a chance.

"Give Mrs. Shelton a message," I said. "Tell her that Donald Lam, a private detective, is registered at the Edgemount Motel and is investigating persons who were at a certain motel on Saturday night, and is particularly interested in all potential witnesses."

"Who is this talking? You say your name is Mr. Knight?"

"Actually," I said, "my real name is Santa Claus. I'm trying to pass on some information that may help Carlotta Shelton. Lam is nobody's fool and he's going to report to his client unless someone stops him. I've stuck my neck way, way out in order to pass on the information. I suppose you're Carlotta Shelton's secretary. You might see that the information reaches her."

I hung up the phone, went back to the Edgemount Motel and went to bed. I didn't expect to get a night's sleep, but I did. Nothing happened.

CHAPTER 10

AT NINE THIRTY the next morning I disguised my voice, called the office and told the switchboard operator I was Harry Carson, a witness Donald Lam had been trying to contact and could I speak with Mr. Lam.

The girl at the switchboard said she'd connect me with Mr. Lam's secretary, and a few moments later I heard Elsie Brand's voice.

I carried on the Harry Carson gag for a while just in case the switchboard operator was listening, but my disguised voice didn't fool Elsie any.

"Where are you now, Mr. . . . . Carson?" she asked.

"On the job," I said.

"Where?"

"It's better for you not to know."

"Bertha is screaming her head off."

"Let her scream."

"She'll fire me if she finds I've been talking with you and didn't tell her where you were."

"Where am I?" I asked.

"Why, I . . . I don't know. You wouldn't tell me."

"That's just the point," I told her. "You don't know. . . . Has Frank Sellers been around the office?"

"Has he been around the office!" she exclaimed. "He's been in twice within the last half-hour."

"And Bertha wants to know where I am, huh?"

"I'll say."

"All right," I said, "you've heard from me. I'm calling from out of town. I said that I wanted very much to talk with Frank Sellers, that I'd tried to trace him and found he was at the office and asked you if he was there. You said that he wasn't, that Bertha Cool wanted to talk with me and I said that I simply couldn't take the time to talk with her until after I had talked with Sellers, that it was important that I get in touch with him, that I had some very important information for him."

"And then what?"

"And then I hung up," I said.

And as I said that, I dropped the telephone back into its cradle and broke the connection.

I settled down to wait.

Waiting can get on your nerves worse than anything in the world. And when you expect something to happen, nothing ever does.

As a friend once said, "If you're expecting an important phone call, don't sit by the telephone, go to the bathroom."

In the early afternoon I called the office again.

"What's new, Elsie?" I said.

"Bertha is having kittens."

"How many?"

"The whole litter."

"People have been telephoning and asking for me?"

"Lots of them."

"Anyone been in?"

"One woman. She said she preferred not to give a name, that she'd wait until you came in."

"A tall blonde with——"

"No, a shapely brunette."

"How old?"

"Twenty-eight or twenty-nine; perhaps thirty."

"A looker?"

"A pippin."

"She wouldn't tell you what she wanted?"

"No."

"And she waited?"

"For well over an hour. For some reason she expected

you to call in. She'd sit out in the outer office for a while and then come in and talk with me, and ask me if you hadn't phoned in."

"And you'd lie to her?"

"I would have, brazenly. Only you didn't call in so I didn't have to."

"What else do you know about her?"

"I can tell you the shade of her stockings, the brand of perfume she uses; I know where she bought her handbag and her shoes. I know that she's been married and divorced, that she is going steady with a boy friend whom she would like to marry, but he hasn't brought the subject up and probably won't. She was frank enough to tell me that there was no reason why he should."

"In other words," I said, "you swapped woman talk."

"That's right."

"What did you tell her about you?"

"Nothing."

"These talks took place in your office or in the outer office?"

"In my office. She sat on the edge of the desk for a while, and got real confidential. . . . She has very nice legs."

"Okay," I said. "She'll probably be back."

I hung up and waited.

Nothing happened.

At three o'clock I called up Bertha Cool.

"Where the hell are you?" Bertha asked.

"Working on a case."

"What case?"

"I don't want to tell you over the phone."

Bertha said, "Sellers has been trying to see you. He wants to talk with you some more."

"I want to see him," I said, "but I have to get a couple more loopholes plugged before I talk with him."

"*I* want to talk with you," Bertha said.

"What about?"

"Donald, I want to be very, very certain we're not holding out a single scrap of information. Sellers has put it on the line. If we don't tell him the name of our client, we are going to lose our license. He says we can tell him off the record if we want to and he'll protect us, but we either tell him or on one excuse or another they'll close us out. He says the police don't let private detectives give them the run-around in murder cases."

"When did he tell you that?"

"Yesterday afternoon and again at nine this morning."

"Did you tell him?"

"No."

"Has he been in this afternoon?"

"No."

"Telephoned?"

"No."

"Then you told him."

"I did no such thing."

"Bertha, you're lying."

"All right. I had to protect our livelihood."

"So that's it," I said. "I wondered why Sellers hadn't found me to put the pressure on me. He didn't have to. You caved in."

"It's all off the record. He'll protect us."

"Baloney!"

"I had to do it. This is one hell of a case. Did you read about what happened in court yesterday?"

"No, what?"

"The district attorney tried to get a continuance because of the death of Ronley Fisher. The defense strenuously objected. The court finally gave the prosecutor's office forty-eight hours to assign a new prosecutor and have him become familiar with the case.

"There's a general feeling around that Fisher had discovered something, some surprise witness whom he intended to call. The D.A. can't afford to lose that Cliffs case, and the police can't afford to have the murder go unsolved. They're turning over every stone and looking under the stone with a magnifying glass."

"Well," I said, "as you so aptly pointed out, you can't expect us to compete with the police."

"Well, you don't need to be so damned smug about it. You could at least assure Frank Sellers you weren't holding out anything, and—well, give him the benefit of *your* thinking."

"He's never wanted the benefit of my thinking so far," I said.

"He does now."

"We'll sleep on it."

"Where are you now?"

"I can't tell you."

"What the hell do you mean, you can't tell me? I'm your partner, you can't——"

"You'd tell Sellers," I said.

"Well, why not?"

"I'm not ready to talk with him."

"Well, he's good and ready to talk with you."

"That's what I'm afraid of," I said, and hung up.

The afternoon dragged on.

Nothing happened.

It was the quiet before the storm.

I turned on the radio. I heard that the trial of Staunton Cliffs and Marilene Curtis for the murder of Cliffs's wife would be resumed tomorrow, that the district attorney had assigned a new trial deputy, that the police were working on a theory that Ronley Fisher had been interviewing a hitherto undiscovered surprise witness in the case when he met his death.

At four o'clock I decided I'd waited long enough. There was a television set in the room and I got down on the floor, fastened the lifted fingerprints to the underside of the television set with Scotch tape.

I'd packed up my bag and was just starting out when there was a gentle knock at the door.

I went to the door and opened it.

I hadn't seen Carlotta Shelton in the flesh but I'd seen pictures of her.

The flesh was *some* flesh.

I pretended to be completely flabbergasted. "Why . . . why . . . I—Good afternoon."

"Good afternoon," she said. "Let me come in, please."

She pushed her way into the room, closed the door behind her, stood with her hands behind her back, looking me over speculatively. Then she smiled.

She was blond, long-legged and vital. She had deep blue eyes and she stood there smiling invitingly.

"Well, Donald," she said.

"You know who I am?"

"Of course I know who you are, Donald, and I know what you're doing. Now tell me, Donald, what are you trying to pin on me? I'm Carlotta Shelton."

"I'm not trying to pin anything on you."

She came toward me, moving with that lithe grace which would make her whistle-bait wherever she went.

"Mind if I sit down?" she asked, and dropped into a chair and crossed her knees.

"You've been asking questions," she said. "You shouldn't do that, Donald."

"You don't get anywhere if you don't ask questions," I said.

"That's right, Donald, but you might get where you didn't want to be. . . . It's hot in here. Mind if I take off my jacket?"

"Go as far as you like," I told her.

"How far would *you* like?"

"Does that matter?"

"It might."

She took off the jacket, came over to me, put her hands around my waist, looked at me with steady candor. "Donald," she said, "you wouldn't hurt a woman, would you?"

"Not if I could help it."

Her hands moved down from my waist to the hips. She pulled me close to her, said, "I'm grateful to my friends, Donald, and I hate my enemies."

"It's a good way to be."

Her hands pulled my hips tightly against her, then suddenly she stepped back, pulled a zipper and slipped out of her dress.

She had on panties, bra and stockings, and she had about the longest, most beautiful pair of legs I had ever seen.

She tossed her dress carelessly on the back of a chair and said, "Donald, I *love* my friends."

She moved toward me with a swaying, seductive motion: She put her left hand around my head, suddenly raked the fingernails of her right hand across my face, stepped back, screamed, picked up a tumbler and hurled it at me.

She raised one hand and ripped at the bra. It dropped from the left shoulder, hung over the right shoulder by a strap.

The door flew open. Three big men entered the room.

"Grab him!" she screamed. "Grab him!"

One of the men aimed a blow at my chin. I tried to duck. His fist glanced off my forehead. Two of the men pinioned my arms. Handcuffs went around my wrists.

"He tried to rape me," she screamed, and fell on the bed, sobbing.

One of the men flashed a star. "All right, Buddy," he said, "what's the idea?"

I felt the blood trickling down my face and onto my shirt.

"You can search me," I said. "She came in here a couple of minutes ago and . . ."

Carlotta struggled to a sitting position, took the dangling bra and pulled it up over her breast. She said, "He tried to blackmail me. He wrote this letter demanding the blackmail. I gave him the money. I was willing to to do that, but when he wanted—when he wanted *me*, I rebelled and then he tried to take me. He said I was in no position to squeal."

"Did he take the money?" one of the men asked.

"Of course he took the money. What do you think he was after?—I mean, that was *one* of the things he was after. He put it in his right-hand hip pocket."

I suddenly remembered her hands on my hips as she pulled me close to her.

One of the men pushed a hand into my hip pocket, came out with some currency folded flat and held with a clip.

"This is the money, all right," he said.

"You better check the numbers and make sure," she said, fumbling with her bra.

Then she got up, and walking as naturally as though she had been fully dressed, moved over to the chair, picked up her dress, shook it out and looked at it ruefully.

There was a tear in it I hadn't seen.

"You're going to have to get me some safety pins," she said. "I can never go out this way."

One of the men said, "Let me see that letter."

She opened the purse which she had placed on the bed when she first came in, took out a letter and handed it to him.

The man pushed the letter under my face. "Ever see this before?" he asked.

It was a sheet of plain stationery, about three inches shorter than ordinary stationery, and the line at the top showed where the letterhead had been folded and then the top had been torn off.

On the paper had been pasted words cut from newspapers and magazines.

The message said: "IF YOU KNOW WHAT'S GOOD FOR YOU, YOU'LL MEET ME, KEEP QUIET, AND BRING THE MONEY."

"I've never seen it before," I said.

"Baloney!" one of the men said.

"Just how do *you* figure in this?" I asked. "What were you doing, standing outside waiting for her to take her clothes off?"

"Don't get smart, Buddy. I'm an officer."

"And the other two?"

"I'm a private detective," one of the men said. "Black Hawk Detective Agency."

"I'm a friend and bodyguard," the other said.

"How much bodyguarding do you do?" I asked.

One of the men slapped me on the face, hard. The blood from the scratch wounds splattered.

"That'll do," the officer said. "No brutality unless he starts something, and if he does, I'll take care of it."

Carlotta said, "Just a slimy specimen of private detective, getting information and then trying to resort to blackmail."

"What information did I have?" I asked.

She smiled sweetly and said, "I know that the police are sufficiently anxious to catch blackmailers so that they'll protect me. I'll tell the district attorney in confidence, and that's it."

I looked at her mocking eyes and said, "All right, suppose *I* tell?"

For a moment there was a swift flicker of panic. Then she said venomously, "You try to besmirch my reputation and I'll *really* have you worked over."

I said, "I'm the one that needs a bodyguard."

The officer said, "Okay, Lam, you're coming with us and get booked."

"For what?"

"Extortion."

"Let's check the numbers on those bills," one of the men said, "while we're all together."

The officer nodded, pulled the bills from his pocket.

There were ten one-hundred-dollar bills. The officer read off the numbers, one of the men checked the list.

The officer put the money in his pocket, said, "Okay, Lam, let's go."

"You know who I am?" I asked.

"Know who you are!" the officer said. "Hell, we know all about you. Remember, your car's parked outside with the registration certificate on the steering post, and you registered under your right name so we can't make a point on that, but we've got you cold on blackmail and probably on attempted rape."

"Let's get this straight," I said. "She came here to pay off. You folks waited outside. At a signal you were to come in and grab me and find the money in my possession—right?"

"What's wrong with that?" the officer said.

I said, "Her dress was over the back of the chair in such a position the tear wouldn't show. Her bra was off. My face was scratched. If you were outside waiting for her signal, why didn't she call you when I started to rip her dress off? Why wait until her bra was ripped off and my face scratched? Why didn't she call you in when the party first started getting rough?"

The officer's eyes faltered.

Carlotta said, "It happened too fast. I was rattled. I forgot the signal."

One of the men said, "That's enough. If you're going to stand there and let him insult her, Officer, I'm going to the chief personally with this. I guess you're familiar with me

—Harden C. Monroe. I flatter myself I have a little influence in this city—in fact, in this state."

Carlotta flashed him a smile that was full of promises.

The officer said to me, "I'm not arresting you for attempted rape—not yet. I'm taking you into custody for blackmail. Come on. We're going places."

They took me down to a police car. The officer checked in with Communications. "I just picked up Lam at the Edgemount Motel," he said. "He had one thousand dollars in marked money on him. Go ahead with the search warrant."

He signed off.

"What search warrant?" I asked.

The officed didn't answer the question.

I was still handcuffed. The officer drove the car. The other two men and Carlotta followed behind in another car.

The officer was in no hurry getting anywhere. He dawdled along, intentionally muffing every traffic signal. Finally he parked his car near the curb and said, "I want to buy a newspaper."

He called a paperboy over, bought a newspaper, sat there reading it.

"Any old time," I said.

"Shut up," he told me.

After a while he called in Communications. "Car Sixteen, special. Any report?"

"Just coming in," the dispatcher said. "I have a message for you. Found torn stationery in office desk."

"Okay, I'm bringing him in."

The officer signed off and from then on we moved right along with the traffic.

We got to Headquarters, they fingerprinted me, booked me, took me upstairs and put me in a cell.

Ten minutes later Frank Sellers walked in.

"Hello, Pint Size," he said.

I said nothing.

"Been trying a little blackmail on the side, eh?"

"What makes you think so?"

He chuckled and said, "I'll show you what makes me think so. See this letter?"

He unfolded the sheet of stationery with the words that had been cut from the magazines and newspapers pasted on it.

"I see it."

"See this piece of torn letterhead?" he said.

He took from his side pocket a piece of letterhead that had been torn from the stationery of Cool & Lam, Investigators. He placed the torn segment against the irregular tear line on top of the letterhead.

The parts fitted perfectly.

"We found this," he said, "in your office desk. God, but you're careless! Why go to all the trouble of cutting out words from a newspaper so they couldn't be traced to you and then pulling a damned fool stunt like folding over your letterhead, pulling off the top part and leaving it in your desk?"

"It does seem rather foolish, doesn't it?" I said.

"That's the worst of you crooks. You always think you're smart and then do some damned fool thing."

"Some very, very foolish thing, I would say," I said. "Almost *too* foolish."

Sellers' eyes narrowed. "What do you mean by that crack?"

"Figure it out for yourself. You've known me a long while. Would I be *that* dumb?"

"Hell, I don't know," Sellers said. "The facts speak for themselves."

"No, they don't," I said. "You speak for the facts, and the facts have been doctored up to suit you."

"What's your story?" he asked.

"I haven't any."

"Well, you'd damned well better get one."

"I'll tell my story when the time comes."

Sellers said, "Look here, Lam, there's no need for you to be so damned cocky. I'd like to be friends with you if you weren't such an arrogant little rooster."

I said, "All right, I demand to be taken before the nearest and most accessible magistrate."

"Now look, Lam, that isn't going to get you anyplace. You're working on something and I have an idea it may—just may—have been connected with that Fisher murder. . . . . Now, you and I have had some differences in the past but there's no reason why we can't be friends now, and I'm in a position where I might—I just might be able to help you."

"You might," I said.

"Now, why did you try to blackmail this babe?"

"I understand they found a thousand dollars in marked currency in my hip pocket."

"That's right. Now tell me, how did it get there?"

"How do you suppose? She put it there when she was standing with her hands on my hips pulling me up close to her."

He laughed and said, "That isn't the way *she* tells it."

I said, "That *isn't* the way she tells it. It's the way I tell it."

"What's your story?"

"I want to be taken to the nearest and most accessible magistrate."

"And without undue delay," he mimicked. "You forgot that."

"You're the one that's forgetting that," I told him.

"You could make this awfully hard on yourself, Pint Size."

"And what you want is to have *me* make it easy on *you*," I said.

"We might make it easy on each other."

I heard the clang of a lock, then shuffling steps in the corridor, then Bertha Cool came striding into view.

"What the hell!" she said.

Sellers whirled. "Hello, Bertha."

Bertha looked at me. "What the hell happened to you?" she asked. "Your face is all bloody, there's blood spattered all over your shirt."

"Police brutality," I said.

"You sonofabitch," Sellers said.

Bertha glowered at him.

"What happened is that he misunderstood a lady," Sellers said.

"You've got a hell of a crust," she said, "having your men come barging into our offices with a search warrant and upsetting everything in the place."

"We didn't upset everything in the place," Sellers said, "we went to Donald's desk first rattle out of the box, and we found what we wanted."

He took the two pieces of stationery from his pocket, matched them up and showed them to Bertha.

Bertha looked at them for a minute, then looked at me. Her eyes were hard and glittering.

"Moreover," Sellers said, "we found a thousand dollars in marked money on him."

"Who scratched you?" Bertha asked me.

"Carlotta Shelton."

"I wouldn't mention her name if I were you," Sellers said to me.

"Why not?"

"She may decide not to prosecute. She may not want the notoriety."

"Tell her that's fine," I said. "Tell her if she doesn't prosecute, I will."

Sellers' eyes wavered.

Bertha said, "What the hell did she scratch you for?"

"He tore her clothes off," Sellers said.

Bertha started to laugh.

"What's funny about it?" Sellers wanted to know.

"Ever try raping a long-legged athlete?" Bertha asked. "An expert at tennis, swimming, water skiing and horseback riding?"

"Can't say that I have," Sellers said.

"Try it sometime," Bertha said. "Come on, Donald, we're getting the hell out of here."

"What do you mean?" Sellers asked.

"Five thousand dollars' bail," Bertha said.

"Who put it up?"

"I did."

"The hell!" Sellers said. "You didn't need to have been so prompt."

"You listen to me, Frank Sellers. Any time you come busting into my offices with a search warrant, you're going to get action, lots of action, and you're going to get it fast. Now then, here's a receipt for the bail. Get that door unlocked and get Donald out of here. Now."

Sellers walked over to the door and yelled, "Hey, Turnkey!"

"Coming," a voice said, and there were more steps in the corridor, the rasping of the lock, then the cell door was opened and I went out.

Bertha said, "My God, you're a mess."

"I know it," I told her. "We'll save the blood-spattered shirt. It's evidence of police brutality."

Sellers said, "I think that bail is altogether too damned low."

Bertha said an unladylike word.

Sellers followed us out to where the property clerk gave me back my property.

Bertha Cool said, "I have one of the agency cars down here."

Sellers said, "Now look, Donald, you *could* get into big trouble on this thing."

"What do you think he's in now?" Bertha asked.

"We're going to keep it out of the papers," Sellers said.

"When does my hearing come up?" I asked.

"Confidentially, I don't think the girl is going to prosecute."

"Let's go," I said to Bertha.

We marched out of the jail.

Sellers watched us go.

Bertha drove the car. "What the hell have you been up to?" she asked.

"I don't know," I told her.

Bertha said, "You're a holy mess. You've got to go to your apartment and get some antiseptic on that face of yours. My God, she certainly did claw you!"

"It was a deliberate plant," I said.

"All right, what caused it?"

I said, "I was messing around."

"Doing what?"

"Checking fingerprints."

"What fingerprints?"

"Those I found in the room in the motel."

"Whose did you find?" she asked.

"So far," I said, "I've found the prints of four or five people."

"Then Carleton Allen wasn't alone in there with the girl?"

"Carleton Allen was in there and so were other people."

"How do you know?"

"I went to his office and got Allen's fingerprints from his steel desk. His prints and Sharon Barker's prints were in the motel unit. And now we come to the part that bothers me."

"What?"

"Ronley Fisher's prints were in the room."

"What!" Bertha exclaimed, her jaw sagging.

I said, "That *could* mean Ronley Fisher, Sharon Barker and Carleton Allen were having a little powwow."

"That's what it has to mean," Bertha said.

"Not necessarily," I told her. "Remember that there's no time clock on a fingerprint. Ronley Fisher could have been in their earlier in the night with a girl friend, and then he left. So then the motel decided to change the sheets and rent the place all over again."

"They do that?" Bertha asked.

"Be your age," I told her.

"I mean places like the Bide-a-wee-bit."

"They all do," I said. "If business if good and they're sure the other people have checked out."

"Then if that happened," Bertha said, "it would mean that Ronley Fisher had a babe with him."

"He had someone with him, and the management of the motel saw him checking out, putting bags in a car and leaving."

"Who would have seen that?"

"The night security officer."

"Have you talked with him?"

"No."

"Why?"

"The police have talked with him. They've turned him inside out."

"Then he would have told the police all about it."

"Would he?"

"Why not?"

"It wouldn't look good for the motel."

"Then you think he lied to the police?"

"It has been done."

"And who do you think was in the room with Ronley Fisher?"

"Drive me out to the motel where I was arrested," I said. "I'll pick up my things and the other agency car. Then we'll talk about that."

"You get your face tended to," Bertha said. "You need some antiseptic on it. Get some peroxide and cotton and you're going to have to put on some clean clothes. Those are all blood-spattered. How did the blood get spattered like that?"

"One of them slapped my face when I was bleeding."

"The sonsofbitches!" Bertha said.

I gave Bertha directions and she drove me out to the Edgemount Motel.

"Come on in," I told her.

Bertha parked the car and followed me in.

The motel manageress came out. "I don't think we care to have you in the motel any more, Mr. Lam."

"I'm here," I said. "My rent's paid until tomorrow."

"We reserve the right to eject objectionable people."

"What's objectionable about me?"

"We don't like to have occupants try to rape women," she said.

"And did I try to rape women?"

"That's what the police say. Also you were blackmailing someone."

"And you're going to eject me for that reason?"

"Yes!" she snapped.

I said to Bertha, "All right, you're a witness. Remember it when we get to court. I'm being ejected on those two grounds, rape and blackmail."

The manageress' face blanched. "Now, wait a minute," she said. "What do you mean? What's this about court?"

I said, "I'll file suit for fifty thousand dollars defamation of character, another fifty thousand dollars for being ejected, and ask for an additional hundred thousand dollars as exemplary damages."

The woman gulped. "How did you get out?" she said.

"Ring up the police and ask them," I told her.

"Step this way, please," she said.

She led the way into the office, took out the key to my unit and handed it to me without a word.

I walked over to the motel unit, opened the door and stood aside for Bertha to go in.

I found the tumbler Carlotta had thrown at me. It had struck the bed, glanced off the wall and rolled down on the floor back of the bed.

I picked it up, keeping my fingers on the inside of the glass, opened my bag, took out my dusting powder and started dusting it.

When I had developed a couple of latent fingerprints, I took out the lifting tape.

"What the hell's all that?" Bertha asked.

"Lifting tape," I said. "I'm going to lift these fingerprints off the glass."

I put on the tape, lifted the fingerprints, mounted the prints on cardboard.

"Go on up to the office," I told Bertha. "I'll clean up and follow along right behind."

Bertha drove her car. I drove mine. When we got to the office, the phone was ringing. Bertha answered, then passed the phone over to me. "For you," she said.

I took the phone, said, "Lam talking."

Frank Sellers said, "I've got good news for you, Pint Size. It pays to co-operate with the police and have friends who are sticking up for you."

"What's the good news?" I asked. "And why the sudden splurge of friendship?"

"The case against you has been dismissed," he said, "and Bertha can get the five thousand dollars' bail back any time she comes up."

"All right," I said, "what about the thousand dollars?"

"The what?"

"The ten one-hundred-dollar bills that were found in my pocket?"

"Why, that's evidence," he said.

"Evidence of what?"

He hesitated. "Evidence of—— Well, hell, it's evidence. The Black Hawk Detective Agency took down the numbers of the bills so there could be no question of the ownership."

"Those bills were paid to me as a fee," I said. "I want them back."

"What the hell are you talking about, Pint Size? That was blackmail."

"Who says it was blackmail?"

"Carlotta Shelton."

"Let her say so in court," I said.

"Why, listen!" Sellers yelled into the phone. "You can't have crust enough to demand that thousand dollars! Why . . . hell's bells, don't press your luck, you damned fool. . . . You'll *force* her to prosecute if you adopt that position."

"Those ten one-hundred-dollar bills were paid me for a fee," I said. "They were taken from my person. I want them back."

"You talk with the D.A."

"I don't know the D.A.," I said. "*You* talk with him. I'm telling you I want that thousand dollars. If you give it to Carlotta, I'll sue you on your bond."

"You sonofabitch!" Sellers said, and hung up.

CHAPTER 11

I LEFT the office and rang up Elsie Brand.

"Donald!" she exclaimed when she heard my voice. "What happened? Bertha said you had been arrested."

"I was arrested."

"And that you were all bloody."

"I was all bloody."

"Oh, Donald!"

"It'll heal up," I told her. "In the meantime, we're fighting minutes. I'm coming by to pick you up and then we're going places. Do you have a date?"

"I—— No."

"Elsie, you're lying."

"I have one but I'm going to break it. I'll explain to him that this is business."

"This," I said, "is business. I'll be by for you in fifteen minutes."

"I'll be ready."

I drove to her place and picked up Elsie. She took one look at my face and was all sympathy. Her fingertips went fluttering over my hairline, smoothing back the hair.

"Donald, it looks terrible."

"It is terrible."

"Why did she scratch you?"

"She wanted to make it look like rape."

"Make *what* look like rape?" Elsie asked.

"The frame-up."

"Donald, did you . . . did you . . . ?"

"No."

"What do we do now?"

I said, "I was framed. That very eager potential client

101

who was waiting for me to come in wasn't waiting for me to come in at all. She knew very well that I was out of the office and was going to stay out of the office, waiting to hear from Carlotta Shelton."

"But why did she wait if she knew you weren't coming in?"

"Because she wanted to steal a piece of stationery, tear off the printed letterhead, drop it in the drawer, and deliver the piece of stationery to Carlotta Shelton."

"Donald, was I that dumb?"

"No," I said. "You were that friendly. You sympathized with the girl because I wasn't in and she seemed to be in trouble."

"She seemed *so* nice."

"And you left her alone in my office?" I asked her.

She started to shake her head, then thought for a moment and said, "Just a few minutes while I went down the hall."

"All right," I said, "the few minutes furnished all the time that was needed. Now we've got to find that girl."

"But, Donald, I don't know her. I've never seen her before. She wouldn't leave a name, and——"

"You'll know her picture if you see it?"

"Why . . . Why, yes. I think so."

"Come on," I said. "You're going to see the picture."

I went to my friend who had charge of the morgue at the newspaper office.

She took one look at me, at the scratches on my face, at Elsie Brand, and smiled knowingly.

Elsie flared up. "Don't look at *me* like that! I wouldn't have laid a hand on him no matter *what* he'd done."

The newspaperwoman was a tall, angular babe in her fifties who had been around. Nobody knew anything about her background. She simply grinned again, then turned to me and said, "With loyalty like that so close to home, why do you go out looking for trouble, Donald?"

"I wasn't looking for trouble," I told her. "Trouble was looking for me."

"What do you want?"

"I want to take a look at the file on Carlotta Shelton."

"That'll be some file," she said.

"I want the photographs," I told her.

"Those are in a separate file. What do you want, bathing suit, sun suit, tennis shorts, riding habit . . . ?"

"I want them all," I said.

She opened a door. We went inside an enclosure and she put us at one of the long tables. After about five minutes she came back with a whole armful of manila envelopes.

"Please don't mix them up," she said, and left.

"Who is she?" Elsie asked.

"Ruth Ritter," I said. "She's a swell scout. No one knows anything about her past. Some sort of a tragedy. She never talks about it. She keeps herself in the background but has an encyclopedic memory and a passion for details."

"She thought *I* scratched you," Elsie said indignantly, and then looked once more sympathetically at my face.

"They won't heal if you keep looking at them," I said.

"Oh, Donald, I just want to take your head and . . . and . . ."

"They'd become infected," I told her.

"Oh, don't be so damned sanitary!" she said.

I opened the first envelope and started spreading out pictures.

Carlotta Shelton was a beautiful girl and she was wonderfully photogenic. Every time she moved she just seemed to fall into poses of natural grace. She loved being photographed and she loved cheesecake.

I passed up all the pictures which showed Carlotta alone and paused over the group pictures.

"That bitch!" Elsie said under her breath.

"You see her?" I asked eagerly.

"No, no. I meant Carlotta."

We went over several dozen pictures. All of a sudden Elsie grabbed at one of the photographs.

"Wait a minute, Donald—I think—I think *that's* the one!"

"Can you be sure?"

"No, I'm not sure, but it—it looks like her."

I turned the picture over and read the caption pasted on the back. "Bathing beauties disport themselves in Salton Sea. Reading from left to right . . ."

I turned the picture over. The one Elsie had picked was the third from the right. She was a good-looking babe, and according to the caption her name was Elaine Paisley.

I went out and called Ruth Ritter.

"Got a file on Elaine Paisley?" I asked.

"How do you spell it?"

I gave her the spelling.

She went back and after a while came back with a rather thin file.

"She's a bathing beauty. Won a contest, had a couple of fill-in parts and is hanging poised on the edge of a career."

"Any pictures?"

"Apparently so."

I opened the envelope.

There were clippings and a couple of photographs. Elsie took one quick look and said, "That's her, Donald. That's the one."

The picture was a close-up of Elaine Paisley sitting on the arm of a chair, her hands clasped around her right knee, her left leg dangling down with lots of nylon.

"You're sure?"

"I'm sure."

I looked through the clippings. There was an address.

I went to the phone book and verified the address.

"Now what?" Elsie asked, her voice tinged with excitement.

"Nothing," I told her, trying to make my voice casual. "We now have some of the information we want, that's all. We'll figure out how to use it later on."

She looked at me sharply, started to say something, then changed her mind.

I gave the envelopes back to Ruth Ritter and drove Elsie home.

"A working girl gets hungry. We *could* have something to eat," she said.

"Later on," I told her.

"You mean tonight?"

"Perhaps."

"I'm hungry *now*, Donald."

"Put some glad rags on."

"Donald, you're stalling for time."

"I don't have any time."

"Donald, I've got some things in my apartment. I could fix up a nice little dinner and you wouldn't have to go out. You're sensitive about your scratched face, aren't you?"

"Yes."

"Will you come back to my apartment?"

"If I can," I told her.

"What do you mean, if you can?"

"I may be in a position where I don't have any choice."

"Then you could call me?"

"I'll try to."

She hesitated a moment, suddenly pulled my head to her and kissed my scratched cheek gently.

"In about an hour," she said.

"Okay," I told her, helped her out of the car and saw her to the door of her apartment house.

As I walked back to the car a figure straightened up from the shadows and Frank Sellers said, "Bertha thought you might be here. . . . Taking your girl home rather early, aren't you, Pint Size?"

"That's my business," I told him.

"That's right," he said, "you got lots of business. You're also in lots of trouble."

"What now?" I asked.

"Income tax," he said.

"You're nuts," I told him.

"You havent paid your income tax. I'm going to have to do something about it."

I said, "Look, Sellers, you quit pushing me around. I'm clean as a cake of soap. I also have some rights as a citizen and I happen to know what they are."

"I'm not trying to push you around," he said, "I'm just doing my duty. I'll take your word for it if you'll put it in writing."

"What?"

"That you don't owe any income tax."

"I'm paid up," I told him.

He handed me a piece of paper. "Write on this, 'I don't owe any income tax,' and sign it."

I took the precaution of dating the paper at the top and wrote as he suggested, and signed it.

I handed it to him.

"Everything okay now?" I asked.

He stepped over so that the street light showed on the paper. Then he chuckled and took another piece of folded paper from his pocket. "All right, Pint Size," he said, "now you *are* in bad."

"What do you mean?"

He showed me the note he was holding. "Take a look at the words, 'income tax'," he said. "They're identical. So you did write this note, 'Police have our office under surveillance. Go to the elevator, go to the floor above ours. There's an income tax expert on that floor. Go in and ask him some questions. Don't go near our offices until we give you the word. Call up later on and find out if the coast is clear.' "

I didn't say anything.

Sellers said, "One of the cleaning women found that note crumpled in the sanded receptacle in front of the elevator on the floor above yours. It just happened that she read it. Then she called us."

I still didn't say anything.

"Well?" Sellers said.

I said, "You think I wrote it?"

"I know damned well you wrote it."

"It's a crime to protect a client?"

"It is in that way, and in this kind of case. That's your license, Pint Size. I hate to lower the boom on you because of Bertha, but you've been asking for it and you've stuck your neck out."

"All right," I said, "I'll make a deal with you. I'll give you the leads that will enable you to step in and clean the case up. I want my client kept out of it and I want it understood nothing is done about our license."

I could see his face light up with eager anticipation but he kept his voice cautious. "I'm not making any promises," he said, "until I see what you've got."

"Where's your car?" I asked.

"I've got it stashed in the alley."

"Get it," I said. "We can go faster in your car than mine. I've got a date in an hour and things to do in the meantime."

"Where do we go?"

"The Edgemount Motel."

"What do you have there?"

"Fingerprints."

"What sort of fingerprints?"

"I lifted them from Unit 27 at the Bide-a-wee-bit Motel."

"I see," he said. "Fingerprints of your client?"

"Fingerprints of my client," I said, "and someone else's fingerprints."

"Whose?"

"Ronley Fisher."

Despite his attempt to keep a poker face, Sellers reacted as though I'd jabbed him with a pin.

"What the hell are you talking about, Pint Size?"

"I'm telling you the truth."

Sellers said, "If Fisher was in that unit—you damned fool, do you realize what that means? It means your client murdered him."

"It doesn't mean any such thing," I said. "It means the motel rented the unit twice. Fisher was there with someone else. They left the place, taking their baggage with them. That gave the motel a vacancy on a Saturday night when business was rushing. The clerk decided to rent the place twice."

Sellers said, "Never mind the theory. You show me Ronley Fisher's fingerprint in that room in the motel and I'll tear the place apart. I'll have the murderer within twenty-four hours. I'll break that case wide open."

"What are we waiting for?" I asked.

Sellers said, "Come on, Pint Size, let's go."

"And if I can deliver, there's nothing more about my license and we can protect our client and——"

"If your client's nose is clean and if you can come up with that fingerprint, you can have just about anything you want. You can write your own ticket. As far as we're concerned, your client could have had a dozen women in there, all at the same time."

"It's a deal," I told him.

We got in Sellers' car and I had to brace myself to keep from being thrown around as he went through traffic. He didn't use the siren and red light but he disregarded all speed limits.

We got to the Edgemount Motel.

I took the key out of my pocket.

Sellers followed me in.

I said, "They're taped to the underside of this television. Tilt it back and I'll get them."

"You tilt it back," Sellers said. "I'll get them."

I heaved on the heavy television set and tilted it back so Sellers, down on his knees, could run his hand down on the underside.

"Tilt it farther back," he said.

I did so.

Sellers straightened. His face was dark.

"Just like I thought," he said. "Another one of your goddam run-arounds."

"You mean there's nothing there?"

"I mean there's nothing there and there never was anything there."

I could feel my jaw sagging.

Sellers, watching the expression on my face, said "You're a good actor, Donald, but it takes more than good acting to put across a run-around like this."

I said, "It's no run-around. Prop something under that leg so we can take a look."

Sellers looked around, found a couple of books, propped them under the leg.

I got down and examined the underside of the television.

"You can see where the tape was placed here," I said. "Look at those two parallel marks."

Sellers seemed completely uninterested. "You're a smart cooky, Lam," he said. "I admit that. I always have admitted it. You took some tape and made marks under here to support your fairy story. You're like the man who says, 'I killed a deer with one shot at five hundred yards. He was standing under that oak tree and if you don't believe it, come on over and I'll show you the oak tree.'"

I said, "I could make a guess as to who has those fingerprints."

"Make a guess as to who is feeding Santa Claus's reindeer," Sellers said. "I'm not interested."

"Listen, Sellers, I'm telling the truth. I——"

"Not interested," Sellers interrupted.

I switched out the lights. We left the place. I put the key in my pocket. Sellers stalked over to his car and got in. I started to get in, but Sellers slammed the door, started the car and left me standing there.

I called a taxicab and gave the address of Elaine Paisley's apartment.

CHAPTER 12

ELAINE PAISLEY'S apartment was in a run-of-the-mill old-style apartment house.

I told the cabbie to pull around the corner and wait.

As I walked into the place I noticed that the stale air had been packed with deodorizers. An elevator rattled and wheezed up to the third floor where Elaine Paisley had her apartment.

I knocked on the door.

"Who is it?" a feminine voice asked.

"Me," I said.

"Oh, I'm so glad you've come," she said, flinging open the door. Then she fell back, looking at me with startled eyes.

She was wearing black stockings, a knitted girdle, a bra and nothing else.

She grabbed up a robe and flung it around her.

I walked into the apartment.

"You can't come in here," she said.

"I'm in."

"Get out."

"We talk first."

"Who are you?"

"The name," I said, "is Donald Lam. You wanted to see me. You were very, very anxious to see me."

"Oh!" she said, her voice flat with dismay.

"So I came to see you," I told her.

She laughed, a little nervous laugh, and said, "Well, you saw me all right."

"Who did you think I was?" I asked.

"You should have given your name when I asked, instead of just saying me."

"Who did you think I was?"

"Does that make any difference?"

"It might."

"Won't you sit down, Mr. Lam?" she asked.

"Thank you," I said. "Were you expecting someone?"

"I was going out," she said.

"With whom?"

"That doesn't make any difference."

"You sure you were going out?"

"You saw that damned girdle," she said. "Any time I put that thing on, I'm going out."

"Uncomfortable?" I asked.

"More or less," she said. "It's the only way you can make stockings behave. . . . I wanted to see you about—about—about a very tricky situation."

"How tricky?"

"Plenty."

"Suppose you tell me about it."

"I may need a bodyguard."

"For how long?"

"I don't know."

"I mean how long out of the day?"

"All the time."

I looked around the one-room apartment with its wall bed.

"Where would I sleep?" I asked.

She laughed nervously and said, "I really hadn't thought about that. What would your rates be?"

"A good man costs fifty bucks a day," I said.

"Fifty dollars?" she exclaimed.

"Uh-huh."

"Well," she said, "I couldn't afford that."

"Why did you need a bodyguard?"

"Use your imagination."

"I haven't any. What's the trouble? Man trouble or woman trouble?" I asked.

"It's—— This is a man." She hesitated a minute and then added, "And a woman."

"What sort of trouble?"

"I . . . I'm afraid that I'm not going to be able to afford a bodyguard."

"And," I told her, "your imagination isn't active enough to think up a factual story that would hold water so you don't dare try."

"What do you mean?"

"I mean," I said, "that you didn't want to employ me at all. You came to my office in order to stick around and snitch a piece of paper. Then you tore off the top part of the letterhead, put it back in my desk and delivered the paper to . . ."

I stopped talking and waited. She was looking at me with wide, startled eyes.

"How in the world did you ever find me?"

"I'm a detective," I said.

She said, "I didn't . . ."

There was a gentle knock on the door of the apartment.

She jumped up, dashed to the door and flung it open.

Harden Monroe, the man who had described himself as Carlotta Shelton's bodyguard and friend, stood on the threshold. "Hi, Beautiful!" he said. "You all ready to . . . ?"

He caught sight of me.

"What the hell!" he said.

I looked up at him and said, "Good evening, Mr. Monroe."

"What the hell are *you* doing here?"

"Miss Paisley," I said, "called at my office earlier in the day. She was very anxious to retain my services. She doesn't seem quite so anxious now."

113

He turned to her. "How did he find you?" he asked.

"I don't know," she said.

"You didn't leave an address, a purse or——?"

"Heavens, no. I'm not that dumb."

"You didn't inadvertently give a right address or do any telephoning or——?"

"No, I tell you," she said. "No! No! No!"

Monroe looked at me with thoughtful speculation. "How did you get here?"

"By automobile."

"Cut the fresh stuff and let's talk turkey. How did you get here?"

"I found Miss Paisley," I said, "because I was looking for the person who had pilfered a sheet of my stationery, torn off the top of the letterhead, put it back in my desk and then used the sheet of stationery to frame me."

He whirled to her. "Did you tell him anything?"

"No."

"Admit anything?"

"Don't be a sap."

"You're accusing Miss Paisley of getting that stationery?" he asked.

I said, "I'm looking for the person who did it."

"All right," he said, "you've come to the wrong place and you've used up your allowance—out!"

"I have some questions I want answered."

"Out!"

"I don't like being framed for . . ."

His big hand caught the front of my shirt and necktie. He jerked me up out of the chair. "Out! I said."

I tried to swing at his jaw but he grabbed my wrist, doubled my arm behind me, pushed it up until I had to move forward in order to ease the pressure and keep from dislocating a shoulder.

She opened the door and he propelled me into the hall.

The door slammed.

I looked back at the door, heard a bolt slide into place.

I went to the rickety elevator, tested my arm to see if I could move it all right and went down to where the cab-driver was waiting.

"A man drove up here about five minutes ago," I said. "A big, broad-shouldered athletic-looking fellow with blond, wavy hair, blue eyes . . ."

"A little over six feet, a hundred and eighty-five, thirty years old," the driver said. "I saw him. What do you want to know about him?"

"Where did he park his car?"

"That convertible," the cabbie said.

"Start your motor," I told him. "If you see him come out of the place, honk your horn, open the door and be ready to run."

"What are you going to do?"

"Take a look at the registration slip on his automobile."

"You an officer?"

"I'm a detective."

"You're not supposed to snoop around someone else's car."

"I'm supposed to get information," I said, "and you're supposed to make money."

"I wouldn't want to get mixed up in anything illegal."

"You aren't."

"How long you going to be?"

"Just a minute."

"I'll watch. If he comes out, I'll open the door and start the motor. I'm not honking any horn."

"Okay," I told him. "I can hear you start the motor. That'll be just as good as a horn."

"Suits me," the driver said. "I've got a right to start the motor any time. Honking a horn is something different. That's a signal. I wouldn't go for that."

I left him, crossed over to the convertible and started prowling.

The registration certificate was in a folder wrapped around the steering post. It showed the owner of the car was Harden C. Monroe. There was nothing in the car that would do me any good.

I tried the glove compartment. It was unlocked.

I took a look inside. There was a flashlight, some maps, a package of cigarettes, and something oblong in the back corner.

I pushed my hand in.

Something stuck to my fingers. I jerked back instinctively, and the Scotch tape pulled the rest of the packet out.

The strip of Scotch tape was sticking to my fingers, leaving the packet dangling.

That packet was the bundle of latent fingerprints I had developed, lifted and stuck to the bottom of the television set at the Edgemount Motel.

I grabbed the packet, slammed the door of the glove compartment shut, closed the door of the car, walked across to where the cabdriver was watching me with interest.

"You take something out of that car?" he asked.

I looked him in the eyes. "No," I said.

"Okay," he told me. "Where do you want to go now?"

I gave him the address of Elsie Brand's apartment house.

I looked at my watch. It had been exactly fifty-two minutes since I'd left her.

I was about on time when I rang the buzzer on Elsie's apartment.

She opened the door. I smelled cooking.

"Ready?" I asked.

"Donald," she said, "I'm broiling you a steak with onion rings and you're having a big potato with lots of sour cream. I'm going to open a bottle of wine and we're going to have a little supper right here. In that way you won't have to go out where people can . . . can stare."

"You're a jewel," I told her, and put my arm around her waist.

She snuggled up against me and tilted her chin.

CHAPTER 13

IT WAS ten o'clock when I left Elsie Brand's apartment. I felt a lot better. Peroxide on my scratches had taken away some of the sting. After the hectic pace I had maintained during the day I felt relaxed, at peace with the world.

As I approached the parked agency car I saw the glow of a cigarette.

A man was seated behind the steering wheel, smoking.

I hesitated.

"Hello, Lam," he said. "Come on in. We're going places."

"Who are you?"

"Police."

"I've been going places with police all day."

"That's fine. Then you can make a perfect record by going all night."

"Suppose I tell you I won't go?"

"Then you're going to come."

The officer moved over in the seat, said, "I'll let you drive, but no funny stuff."

"Look," I told him, "I've been with Sergeant Sellers, I've told him all I know, I——"

"Now look, Lam," the officer interrupted, "I gave you a break. I got here fifteen minutes ago. I could have dragged you out of that apartment, but I was considerate. I decided to give you half an hour. Sellers said he wanted to have you and Bertha Cool at his office at ten-thirty. I could have taken you in and left you cooling your heels. As it was, I gave you a break and let you alone. That's all the thanks I get."

"All right," I told him, "thanks."

"That's better."

I started the car and drove to Headquarters. We arrived at ten-twenty-five.

Bertha was waiting in Sellers' office. Sellers had been talking with her and she was frightened.

The officer brought me in.

"Hello, Pint Size," Sellers said.

"Well, well," I told him, with feigned surprise. "Fancy meeting *you* here."

Sellers said to Bertha, "Always full of wisecracks. He's cost you your license and he has to clown it up to the end."

Sellers turned to the officer. "This guy clean?" he asked.

"I didn't frisk him."

Sellers frowned. "Frisk the sonofabitch," he said.

The officer said, "Put up your hands, Lam."

"Now look," I told him, "you've got no right to——"

"I know, I know," Sellers said, "but we can book you on suspicion or as a material witness, and everything you've got will be put in an envelope and given to the property clerk and then we can release you an hour later and you can get your stuff back. Which way would you prefer?"

I held up my hands.

The officer's hands ran down along my body, then stopped as they came to the coat pocket. "Something in here," he said, and pulled out the packet of fingerprints.

"What?" Sellers asked.

"It's none of your business," I said. "It's not a weapon and——"

"Pass it over," Sellers said.

The officer passed it over.

Sellers undid the wrappings, looked at the lifted fingerprints. "Well, well, what do you know!" he said.

Sellers turned to Bertha Cool. "See what I mean,

119

Bertha? I told you the guy was holding out on us. That's typical of the way he works. He pretended to take me into his confidence, tell me all about the fingerprints, take me out to the Edgemount Motel so he could deliver them to me, and then be *so* surprised when he found out they were gone. Actually he had them all the time, stashed away."

"I didn't have them all the time," I said. "I just got them."

Sellers grinned. "You should be writing movie scenarios, Donald, you've got the most imaginative mind and the fastest fund of fiction I know anything about. Come on now, sit down and tell us, just how did you get these?"

I said, "I'll level with you. It won't do any good but I'll level with you."

"Go on, get to the germ of the plot," Sellers said. "You don't usually have to spar for time like this."

"I'm not sparring for time."

"Then talk."

I said, "I was framed on that blackmail business. Carlotta Shelton framed me. She had a friend get a sheet of stationery from my office, tear off the letterhead, drop it in the desk, then bring the sheet to her.

"Carlotta, probably with the help of her boy friend, Harden C. Monroe, cut up newspapers and magazines so they could piece together the words of a blackmail letter. They pasted it on the sheet of paper. Then they got a private detective, and the private detective got a police officer.

"Once they had the trap all set they went to the Edgemount Motel. Carlotta came in by herself. She was all honey and endearment. She made passes at me and slipped the ten one-hundred-dollar bills into my hip pocket while she was pressing her hips up against mine.

"She had carefully ripped her dress before she came in, holding the folds so the tear wouldn't show. Then she

120

raked her fingernails across my face, unzipped the dress, tore off her bra and screamed."

"I know, I know," Sellers said. "We hear this every time a guy gets picked up for blackmail or attempted rape. The girl was the aggressor, she was trying to rape him. He was manfully resisting and then the girl tore her clothes off."

"That doesn't mean that it couldn't happen that way," I said.

"That's right," Sellers said, "but it does mean that we just aren't impressed with the story. It's like the woman who's having a fight with her husband and then everything blacks out and the next thing she knows, John is lying on the floor and she has a gun in her hand and is screaming, 'John, John, speak to me,' but John can't speak because he's dead."

"Never mind all this crap," Bertha said to Sellers. "I'm up past my bedtime. I'm going to get the straight of this thing."

She turned to me. "And then I'm going to grab a life preserver," she said. "You can bind the partnership with legal obligations but you can't jeopardize *my* career with a lot of crooked stuff."

Sellers said, "I'll throw you a life preserver, Bertha, if your nose is clean. That's why I want to get this thing straight. Go on, Lam, start talking, and this time use words that mean something."

I said, "Since I didn't send Carlotta Shelton that letter, I knew she had to arrange to get my letterhead and leave a plant in my desk through some friend.

"I asked Elsie Brand, my secretary, about people who had been hanging around the office and she told me about this girl who had been so anxious to see me that she waited and waited for me to come in.

"I got Elsie and we went to the newspaper morgue. We went through the photographs of Carlotta Shelton, looking

121

for group pictures of her with friends. We found a picture of Elaine Paisley and that looked like the one we wanted. So then we got the Elaine Paisley file where there were clear photographs and she was the one, all right.

"So I went to Elaine Paisley's apartment and asked her what it was she was so anxious to see me about. I caught her off guard and I would have got somewhere if Harden Monroe hadn't come walking in."

Sellers' eyes showed interest. "What did Harden Monroe want?" he asked.

"I don't know what he wanted," I said, "but I know what he didn't want. He found me there, threw me out of the place, and by this time has stiffened Elaine Paisley up so that nobody will ever get an admission out of her now."

Sellers was studying the lifted fingerprints on his desk.

"I see, I see," he said in an absent-minded tone of voice. "Your secretary identified Elaine Paisley as being the one who was hanging around your office."

"That's right."

"Now, these fingerprints, Lam, why didn't you tell me you had them? Why go to all that trouble giving me a run-around?"

"I told you I had them. I also told you they had been taken from the place where I'd concealed them."

"A nice run-around," Sellers said. "That's what I don't like about you, Donald. Bertha is willing to co-operate, but you give the officers a run-around so you can take a short cut where you want to go."

I said, "I don't give you a run-around, and any time I take a short cut I give the police a chance to come along by the same route. If you won't accept the invitation, that's the best I can do."

"I know, I know," Sellers said. "You love to tell us how to run our business. We like to run it our own way. Now tell me about these fingerprints, Donald."

I said, "Monroe threw me out of Paisley's apartment. He was driving a sports model and I decided to take a look in it."

"Why?"

"Because," I said, "somebody had to go back to my place at the Edgemount Motel and steal those fingerprints. It couldn't have been Carlotta Shelton because she had to go up to Headquarters to tell her version of the assault with intent to commit rape. It couldn't have been the detective because she didn't want him to know that much. It wasn't the police officer or you'd have known about it. Therefore, out of the four people who were staging that scene at the Edgemount Motel, Monroe had to be the guy. I took a look in the glove compartment of his convertible and struck pay dirt."

Sellers drummed with his fingers on the desk, looked at his wrist watch, picked up a cigar, thrust it into his mouth without lighting it. His eyes narrowed.

"The interesting thing about your stories, Pint Size, is that they always sound so damned plausible that someone who didn't know his way around would be inclined to buy them. . . . Now look, I know you don't want to drag your secretary into this thing if it's a phony. Are you telling me the truth about Elaine Paisley and the way your secretary got her spotted?"

"That's the truth," I said. "You can check it all the way down the line."

"Harden Monroe, huh?" Sellers asked.

I didn't say anything.

"Now, these latent fingerprints that you've lifted," Sellers said. "You put names on the lifts. They're in your handwriting, all right. You've got Fisher, you've got someone you've simply put on here as C. A.—— Now, who's C. A.?"

"Our client."

"Tell him who the client is," Bertha Cool said. "This is

a murder rap and we're sitting in the middle. We can protect our client just so far and after that . . ."

Sellers held up his hand, palm toward Bertha. "Hold it, Bertha."

Bertha stopped talking and glared.

"I'll give you a break on that," Sellers said. "You don't need to tell us who he is. We know."

"You know," I said, "because you've already shaken Bertha down for the information, and she's putting on an act to make it look good."

The door opened and an officer escorted a frightened, white-faced Carleton Allen into the room.

Sellers grinned at me. "Go on, Pint Size, don't stop talking now."

I settled down in the chair, said nothing.

Carleton Allen looked at Sellers, at Bertha and me, and said, "You have betrayed me. You——"

"Shut up," I said, "before you betray yourself."

Sellers grinned and said to Allen, "Oh, so you know these people, do you?"

Allen thought for a minute, then said, "Yes, I know them. What's the meaning of this? You can't drag me up here without any charge having been placed against me."

"We can't, eh?" Sellers asked.

"That's right, you can't."

"Well, you're here, aren't you?"

Allen said nothing.

"Now I'll tell you why you're here," Sellers said, "and *you* can do the talking."

Sellers took an envelope from his pocket. From the envelope he took the piece of paper on which I had written my note to Allen.

Sellers said, "You'll notice this paper has been crumpled and thrown away. We retrieved it and smoothed it out.

"Now then, Allen, you threw this message away. You put it on top of the sand in the brass refuse container in front of the elevator. The one on the floor above where Cool and Lam have their offices.

"The records of the income tax expert you were told to consult show that there was only one new client who came in to consult him in the morning.

"Evidently you haven't had much experience in this sort of thing because while you were talking with the income tax expert, you gave him your real name and address and asked him some rather inane questions about income tax law and paid him a twenty-dollar fee for his advice.

"Now then, suppose you start doing some talking."

Allen moistened his lips with the tip of his tongue, looked helplessly from Sellers to Bertha Cool, from Bertha Cool to me.

I made a surreptitious gesture, raising my hand to my face and then moving my elevated forefinger across my lips, signaling him to keep quiet.

He didn't catch the signal or didn't pay any attention to it.

"Well?" Sellers asked.

"All right," Allen said, "I'm in a position where I couldn't afford to be involved in a scandal. I was at the Bide-a-wee-bit Motel Saturday night with a dame. Things didn't go right and I got drunk and passed out. Later on I found that the police were checking all registrations at that motel and I couldn't afford to be tagged. I hired Donald Lam to go back Monday night and take my place.

"He did it. Tuesday morning I telephoned the firm and congratulated them on the way they had handled the case. I was on my way in to make an adjustment and settle up when Lam brushed against me in the lobby and handed me this note. I read it in the elevator, went on up to the income tax expert and asked him some questions and went home."

"You were at the motel Saturday night?"

"Yes."

"With a dame?"

"Yes."

"Who?"

"Sharon Barker, the hostess at the Cock and Thistle cocktail bar."

"You're married?"

"Yes."

"You were playing around?"

"No. I—well, I don't know exactly how this did happen. I had chatted with her once or twice before but this time she was definitely on the make and I was at loose ends that night and I felt flattered, and—well, that's the way it was."

"And what happened after you got to the motel?"

"The party went sour."

"What did she do?"

"Walked out on me."

"What did you do?"

"Got drunk, passed out, came to with a hang-over, got up and drove home."

"What time?"

"That I drove home?"

"Yes."

"Just before daylight. Daylight was breaking just as I got home."

"Your car?"

"Yes."

"Then what?"

"Then nothing until I heard that the police were checking on all registrations at the motel and I got in a panic. I got hold of Sharon and asked her if she'd help me with a cover-up. She wanted to know what I had in mind. I told her I wanted to get someone to use the same name under which we had registered and answer the police questions."

"She agreed?"

"On one condition. I had to arrange with Donald Lam to be the detective who substituted for me. She'd seen him and liked him. She said she'd spend the night with him but she wasn't going to do it with just any beefy detective that I'd pick out. That put me on a spot. I had to have Lam. I couldn't get along with anybody else."

Sellers turned to me. "If you'd told me all this, we'd have protected your client and we'd have protected you. Now then, you've got yourself in a hell of a jam, Pint Size. If Bertha wants to dissolve the partnership and carry on by herself we'll try to protect her, but as far as you're concerned you're finished as a private detective. You've got no more license than a jack rabbit."

Sellers picked up the latent fingerprints which I had lifted. "Now then, how about these fingerprints?"

I said, "You've got the fingerprints of Sharon Barker. You've got the fingerprints of Ronley Fisher. You've got fingerprints that I think are those of Carlotta Shelton. I haven't had a chance to check them."

"This whole damned thing could be a plant," Sellers said, "but if Ronley Fisher was in that room, it's a great big development in the case."

"He wasn't in the room," Carleton Allen said. "No one was there except Sharon and me."

Sellers looked at me thoughtfully. "The little bastard could plant evidence all right and . . ."

Sellers turned to the officer. "Take this guy out and fingerprint him," he said, jerking his head toward Carleton Allen. "Bring back the prints and I'll make a check and see whether that part of it is okay."

He picked up a phone and said, "Get me the fingerprints of Ronley Fisher. I want them in here right away. There's a copy on file in the office."

"I object to being fingerprinted," Allen said. "That is . . ."

Sellers jerked his head toward the door.

The officer clamped fingers on Allen's arm and said, "Let's go. You don't know when you're well off. Do you want your picture in the papers?"

"Good God, no," Allen said.

"Well, you're taking the best way to get the publicity you seem to be trying to avoid."

Allen went with him without any more argument.

Bertha said to Sellers, "Now, wait a minute, Frank. If Donald is telling the truth about this, you've got no right trying to go for our license."

"The hell I haven't!" Sellers said. "Solving murder cases is for the police, not for private agencies. The minute Donald got Ronley Fisher's fingerprints out of that room he should have broken all speed records getting up here to report to me."

I said, "I telephoned the office several times and left word that I wanted to talk with you."

"He did that," Bertha said.

"But you didn't telephone Headquarters and try to get in touch with me," Sellers said.

"No."

"Why not?" he asked, chewing on the unlit cigar.

"Because," I said, "I thought you'd want to have the credit. I know how things are up here in the department. On a big case of this sort there are probably half a dozen people who would stab you in the back in order to get the credit for breaking the case."

Sellers' eyes narrowed. He looked at me thoughtfully. "All that devotion for a friend," he said sarcastically.

"All that devotion for a friend," I told him. "I thought you were giving me a break and I was going to give you one."

"Now then," Sellers went on, "you *lifted* those fingerprints. No one can prove those fingerprints were in that room except you. If you'd left them in place and a police photographer could have photographed the fingerprints, that would have been evidence. As it is, you've stuck your neck out and a defense attorney would knock you out of the ball park."

I said, "I had no idea they were Fisher's fingerprints. I was simply taking the precaution of getting fingerprints in order to protect myself."

"When did you find out they were Fisher's prints?"

"When I got his prints from the coroner's office."

"Why did you go to the coroner's office to get Fisher's prints?"

"I wanted to show that none of the fingerprints in the apartment had anything to do with the Fisher case and I had to get his prints to prove that none of the latents were his. Then to my surprise I got a match."

"You're lying," Sellers said. "You had a hunch."

"All right, I'm lying. I had a hunch."

"Then was when you should have called me."

"Then was when you'd have laughed at me, and told me to go fly a kite."

Sellers chewed on the cigar.

An officer came in with a set of fingerprints. Sellers took a magnifying glass and the fingerprints and started comparing.

He kept his face expressionless but started chewing his cigar more and more rapidly. The end of the unlit cigar bobbed up and down like a pendulum.

He straightened up, put down the magnifying glass, looked at me and said, "You little bastard, you've got something and I don't know what. These fingerprints that you've marked 'Fisher' match."

"I told you they matched."

"I know you told me," Sellers said. "You've told me lots of things. Some of them I believe. Some of them I don't. I'm not going to buy your story except as it proves itself step by step."

"What do you think I'm trying to sell you?" I asked.

"Frankly I don't know," Sellers said. "But I know that Bertha's said you're a brainy little bastard so many times that it's gone to your head. You've got so you believe it by this time. You're trying to pull a fast one. I don't know what it is, but I'm not going to buy it and I'm going to put enough grease on your fingers so you can't throw any curves across the plate."

The officer who had Carleton Allen in custody came in with fingerprints.

Sellers took those fingerprints, selected some of my lifts, studied them with the glass, then frowned. He checked once more. Then he put down the glass, looked at me, took the cigar out of his mouth, held it between his two fingers and made little jabbing gestures toward me with it to give emphasis to his words.

"Now then, you pint-sized bastard," he said, "we've got you over a barrel. You were fabricating this whole business, trying to get a story that would get you off the hook."

"What are you talking about?" I asked.

"Those Carleton Allen fingerprints," he said. "They don't match."

"Don't match!" I exclaimed.

"That's right."

I said, "I *couldn't* have made a mistake on those."

"That's the way I feel about it," Sellers said. "You didn't make any *mistake*. You tried to get smart. You were fixing up a story that you were going to sell us so you could get yourself off the hook. You've been fabricating evidence and——"

"There are some latents I lifted in there on which I don't have a match," I said. "I don't know whose they are. Try those. Maybe one of those is Allen's fingerprint. I may have had a wrong steer."

Sellers thought for a moment, then put the soggy cigar back in his mouth and started checking latents.

130

"Let me help," I said. "I——"

"Go to hell," Sellers said, without looking up. "You're not getting near these latents. You're not touching anything."

Ten minutes later Sellers looked up and shook his head. "No match," he said. "None of Allen's prints."

Bertha said, "But Allen admits being there. He——"

"Sure he does," Sellers said. "That's the thing that proves this whole set of fingerprints is a phony, a piece of evidence concocted out of blue sky by Donald to get himself off the hook."

Sellers turned to me. "All right, Pint Size, you've asked for it and you're going to get it."

"Now look," Bertha said, "there's something funny about this whole business. Donald isn't concocting evidence like that."

"I thought you were going to dissolve the partnership and keep your nose clean," Sellers said.

"I'm going to get a fair deal," Bertha said, "and I'm going to see that Donald gets one."

"I'll tell you what's going to happen to Donald," Sellers said. "Do you know what a drunk tank is like?"

Bertha's face showed she wasn't following Sellers' thinking.

"I'll tell you what it's like," Sellers said. "They pick up drunks off the street and throw them into this tank. The guys get sick. They upchuck all over themselves and all over each other. They scream and holler and snore and vomit. They fight and cuss and lose all control.

"Now, your dear little Donald is going to be put in the drunk tank. In the morning perhaps he can prove he wasn't drunk, but right now I think he's drunk. Otherwise he wouldn't claim that he had Carleton Allen's fingerprints. He wouldn't claim that he got all these lifted latents from that room in the Bide-a-wee-bit Motel.

"Maybe Donald will have to stay in that drunk tank for

131

two or three days before he sobers up. When he gets so he can tell me a story about these fingerprints I'll believe, I'll let him out."

Bertha said, "You can't do it, Frank."

"The hell I can't. You just watch me."

"All right," Bertha said, "you can't get away with it."

"Who's going to stop me?" Sellers asked, glaring at her.

"I am," she said, glaring right back.

Sellers said, "Now you listen to me, Bertha Cool. You've teamed up with this smart little bastard and he's had you in hot water ever since you started the partnership. He's always cutting corners. He's got you in a spot now where your license doesn't stand as much chance as a snowball in hell. I'm giving you a chance to save yourself. I'm throwing you a life preserver just on account of old-time friendship. You get smart and grab it and hang onto it, and I'll see that you come out all right. You can go back to a respectable, quiet detective agency practice and quit this business. You weren't intended for that high-pressure kind of stuff anyway."

Bertha said, "There's something fishy about this whole business. You throw Donald in the drunk tank and I don't want any life preserver."

Sellers said, "You've just lost a license, Mrs. Bertha Cool."

"And you can go to hell, you arrogant sonofabitch!" Bertha screamed at him. "You may not know it, but you've just lost your job."

Sellers said to one of the officers, "Take her out. Take Pint Size down to the drunk tank. He's pickled."

CHAPTER 14

THE drunk tank was all that Sergeant Sellers had promised.

When they first threw me in there weren't too many people, and they weren't in too bad shape.

One of them had been arrested for drunk driving. He was fairly well dressed and he had a crying jag thinking of what was going to happen to his good name, to his wife and children, and put in his time being tearfully repentant.

Then there was the sociable drunk who wanted to keep talking and talking and shaking hands and shaking hands.

He'd tell his story over and over. He'd pledge undying friendship. He'd shake hands. Then he'd shake hands all over again. Then he'd start talking and tell the same old story.

There was one belligerent drunk who wanted to fight everybody in the tank, but he soon went to sleep.

Along at one or two o'clock in the morning the worst cases began to come in.

The place was just a big square cage with a floor of cement and a drain in the middle of the floor so that in the morning after the drunks had left, the place could be washed out with a hose.

Ordinarily liquids would drain toward the center of the floor and go down the drain, but along about three o'clock when the place got crowded a couple of inert bodies plugged the grated drain and liquids began to seep all over the place. The sour odor of vomit penetrated everything.

I got in a corner, tried to avoid the seeping liquids and my fellow man. Once or twice I even dozed off.

At six o'clock in the morning they brought in a hot liquid that was supposed to be coffee. Bleary-eyed wrecks reached for the cups with shaking hands.

At eight-thirty they called the crew out to go to court but when I tried to join the procession I was pushed back.

"You're too drunk to go to court," the man said. "You stay here."

I was left with four others, sodden wrecks who were too filthy and unpresentable to be taken anywhere.

At nine o'clock my name was called.

I went over to the door of the tank.

A man said, "This way," and opened the door. I went out.

The property clerk gave me back the things that had been taken from me. The officer put me in an elevator. We wound up in Frank Sellers' office.

Sellers sat behind the desk.

Bertha Cool, looking as grim as a bull dog guarding a shank bone, sat on one side of the room by a hard-faced individual with piercing gray eyes.

Bertha introduced him. "Dawson Cecil, our attorney," she said.

Cecil shook hands.

Sellers said, "Now look, let's get this thing straight. I wasn't picking on the guy. I thought he was drunk. He had to be, the claims he was making. I ordered him put in the drunk tank but I intended to have him transferred out of there just as soon as we could have somebody make a check to see if it was safe for him to be transferred or released."

"And you forgot it," Cecil said.

"I didn't forget it," Sellers said. "Not in that sense of the word, but there was just too much stuff on my mind and—damn it, I'm working on a murder case. I've been working the clock around, grabbing little snatches of fitful

134

sleep whenever I could. I can't keep a lot of details in my mind."

I said to Cecil, "His memory wasn't so overworked that he forgot to leave instructions that I was to be put back in the tank this morning when they took the men out to court. He'd left word that I would be too drunk to go to court and I was to be put back for another twenty-four hours."

Sellers said hastily, "Now, that's something you'll have to take up with the fellow who's in charge of the tank. I didn't leave any instructions like that at all. I simply said to keep you there until you were good and sober."

Sellers turned to face me and said, "Why do you want to hold a grudge, Donald? I have co-operated with you in the past and I'm willing to do it again whenever I can."

"Why so friendly all of a sudden?" I asked.

Bertha Cool indicated several sheets of paper on Sellers' desk. "Because Elaine Paisley made a complete confession of what she'd done," she said. "Elaine was sent to the office by Carlotta Shelton, with instructions to get one of our letterheads, tear off the printed part at the top in an irregular manner so the torn piece would be identified, to leave part with the printing on it in your desk and bring the sheet to her.

"She went up to the office and hung around until she had a chance to follow instructions. She gave the sheet to Carlotta. It was a blank sheet of paper when she gave it to Carlotta. Carlotta put the printing on it. Elaine Paisley didn't know anything about that."

"And what does Carlotta say now?" I asked.

"Carlotta Shelton and Harden Monroe seem to have disappeared," Cecil said. "They can't be located."

"We'll find them," Sellers promised.

"Right now," Cecil said, "we're talking about you, Mr. Lam. There are civil rights departments who are interested in learning about police brutality. If you were tossed into the drunk tank just in order to make you talk, there's going to be a stink about this thing that will have Sellers back pounding pavements."

"Now, you just keep your shirt on," Sellers said to the attorney. "I know Bertha and I know Donald Lam. They're all right. They're not going to make things rough for an officer. They realize there are times when we get on opposite sides of the fence. We each have our obligations. They're fair and reasonable and you had better be the same way."

Cecil said, "We'll probably file a civil suit for a hundred and fifty thousand bucks and demand an investigation by the Commission."

Sellers looked at Bertha. "Look, Bertha, we've always been friends."

"We have been," Bertha said, "but lately you've been taking funny ways of showing it."

"You know as well as I do a firm of detectives can't get along in this town if it has police opposition," Sellers said.

Cecil said, "Remember that statement. I consider it as a threat, an attempt to get you to waive your civil rights in order to let him out of a hole."

"That wasn't a threat," Sellers said, "that was merely a statement of fact."

"What about this statement from Elaine Paisley?" I asked Bertha Cool.

Sellers said, "It probably isn't worth the paper it was written on. It was probably the result of force and coercion."

"How would I be in a position to exert any force or any coercion?" Bertha asked. "I'm just a private citizen."

"There was no force or coercion whatever," Cecil said. "I have the original affidavit in my possession, subscribed and sworn to before me as a notary public by Elaine Paisley at eight o'clock this morning. I particularly asked her if there had been any coercion, any persuasion, any inducements held out, or any hope of reward. My secretary took down the entire conversation."

Sellers said, "Of course this puts Lam in a position to do something about the Carlotta Shelton affair but it doesn't mean a thing to the police. There's no criminal offense there."

"Extortion, blackmail, making a false report to the police," Cecil said. "You could find plenty of ground for police interference when Miss Shelton was making a complaint against Lam. Now you seem to be singularly aloof."

"All right, all right," Sellers said. "Go on, rub it in. Now come on down to earth and tell me what it is you want."

I caught Cecil's eye. "Right now," I said, "I don't think there is any good to be gained by talking this thing over with Sergeant Sellers. After all, we intend to sue him and you're an attorney at law and you should discuss the matter with Sellers' attorney, not with Sellers himself.

"Moreover, I think we should all have an opportunity to cool off before we discuss anything."

I flashed Cecil a quick wink.

Cecil immediately got to his feet. "If that's the way you feel about it, Lam," he said, "that's the way it's going to be. We have protested the outrage to Sergeant Sellers and we're demanding our rights. I feel that you should have a medical examination. There is every possibility that those scratches on your face have become infected.

"Due to the statement made by Elaine Paisley it is now readily apparent that Carlotta Shelton framed this whole deal in order to discredit you and hamper any investigation you might be making."

Sellers said, "Look, you can't get blood out of a turnip. I'm a cop. I've got nothing. Carlotta Shelton is society stuff. Why don't you go after her and leave me alone?"

"We're going after everyone," Cecil said, "and we're

not precluding the possibility that there was some collusion between you and Carlotta Shelton. You will probably be made a defendant in that suit as well as in the suit against you for unlawful arrest, malicious prosecution and the abuse of the powers vested in you."

With that, Cecil marched over to the door and held it open.

Bertha Cool sailed majestically through and I followed.

Sellers sat there at the desk, holding the copy of the statement from Elaine Paisley and looking as though his breakfast wasn't digesting.

In the corridor Bertha looked at me and said, "My God, you're a mess."

"I'm a mess," I told her. "I'm going home and clean up."

"Say nothing to anyone," Cecil cautioned. "The reporters will be asking you about the suit we intend to file. Refer everyone to me."

Bertha Cool said, "We aren't actually going to file any suit unless we have to. We're just getting Sellers off our backs."

"That's all right with Sellers," Cecil said, "but this Shelton business is something else again."

I said, "I'm going home and get these clothes off, take a bath, a shampoo and a shave."

"God knows you need them," Bertha said.

Cecil said, "It would be just as well if you didn't show up at the office today, Lam, and it's advisable for you not to be too accessible to reporters."

"I won't be accessible to anyone," I told him.

We went down to the main entrance. Cecil shook hands and left.

I turned to Bertha. "I'm going to keep under cover," I told her. "I'll call in every once in a while to see what's new, but there won't be anyplace where you or anyone else can get in touch with me."

"Keep your nose clean," Bertha cautioned. "Dawson Cecil makes it sound good but we're skating on thin ice."

"What happened with Elaine Paisley?" I asked.

Bertha said, "I picked up enough in Sellers' office from what you said to know what the score was. I went down to that woman's apartment. She was out and didn't get in until one o'clock in the morning. When she got in I went to work on her. By two o'clock she was all caved in. I took her to a hotel, kept her awake all night, got hold of Dawson first thing this morning, and had him take Elaine Paisley's affidavit. Then we got hold of Sellers."

"How much work did you have to do on Elaine Paisley?" I asked.

"Not too much," Bertha said. "I manhandled her once when she was going to have me thrown out."

I said, "If she can show black-and-blue marks and——"

"Don't be silly," Bertha said. "I thought about that. I threw the little bitch down on the bed and sat on her stomach while I was talking to her. After a couple of hours she listened."

CHAPTER 15

IT TOOK me a while to get myself cleaned up so that I'd be presentable.

Having had a shampoo, shave and a soak in the bathtub, I knew that I didn't smell; nevertheless whenever my nostrils got a whiff of any strong odor it automatically registered as the odor of the drunk tank and made me think I was carrying the stench with me.

I was dog tired, but I got in the agency heap and drove out to Carleton Allen's office.

The cute secretary was on duty, only this time she was acidly efficient.

"Good morning, Mr. Lam," she said. "Did you have an appointment with Mr. Allen?"

I said, "No appointment with Mr. Allen and I don't want to see him. I want to see Mr. Getchell."

"Oh, you'd have to have an appointment with Mr. Getchell. You——"

I walked past her and opened the door of the office marked *Marvin Getchell*.

She jumped up and ran after me. "You can't do that," she said.

Getchell looked up from his desk.

He was a big, broad-shouldered, grizzled figure of a man. He looked tough, exceedingly fit and very virile.

He was a man in his early fifties with the build of a wrestler and when I entered the office he said to the secretary, "What's all this, Lorraine?"

"He forced his way in," she said. "He . . ."

Getchell got up and pushed his chair back. "I'll take

care of him," he said, and came around the desk, moving with quick steps. "I'll force his way *out*."

Lorraine Beal said quickly. "His name is Donald Lam. He came in the day before yesterday to see Mr. Allen and . . ."

Getchell stopped midstride, took hold of the corner of the desk and said, "Lam, eh?"

"That's right," I said.

"Go out and close the door," he said to the secretary. "I'll take care of this personally."

The door closed.

Getchell towered above me, looking at me with steady, gray, belligerent eyes.

"All right, Lam," he said, "what the hell do you think you're doing?"

"I think I'm protecting a client," I said.

"All right then, go out in the outer office, wait until your client sends for you and then protect him. Don't come busting in here."

I said, "The worst of it is, I fell for that line of hooey once."

"What do you mean, a line of hooey?"

I said, "I didn't fall for it all the way. I thought there was something suspicious about it. I just wanted to check so I got in Carleton Allen's office, took fingerprints off the metal strip around the edge of his desk and compared them with the prints I found in the motel unit. When I got a match, I assumed that Allen had actually been there in the unit. The real explanation didn't occur to me until I found out they weren't Allen's prints."

Getchell studied me thoughtfully for a minute, then walked back behind the desk and seated himself in the swivel chair.

"Sit down, Lam," he invited.

I said, "We may not have very much time."

"Why not?"

"The police aren't entirely dumb."

"You've been to the police?"

"The police have been to me."

He opened a drawer, took out a checkbook, held his desk pen poised over the check, said, "All right, what do you want?"

"I want the truth, to begin with."

"It might be better if you had money."

"I want the truth, *to begin with*," I repeated.

He put down the desk pen, closed the checkbook, said, "I'm a widower."

I nodded.

"I'm also a man."

Again I nodded.

He said, "I met Sharon Barker down at the cocktail lounge. She's cute. I liked her. We went out together."

"How many times?"

"Does it matter?"

"Not really."

"All right," he said. "We went out together. Saturday night we went to the Bide-a-wee-bit Motel after she got off work and we had a little bite to eat. She registered. I'm not entirely unknown and I like to keep out of sight in registration offices. She registered us as Mr. and Mrs. Carleton Blewett of San Francisco, got the key and we went to the motel.

"We ordered some setups and for some reason the house detective was a little suspicious. When the setups arrived, he brought them himself."

"That bothered you?"

"Not too much. I hold a first mortgage on the joint and it should be run to make money, not make trouble. I resolved to see that a new house detective was employed; in fact, I see no reason for having what they call a security officer at a motel of that sort anyway."

"What happened after that?" I asked.

142

"There was a knock at the door," he said, and paused.

"Go on."

"Lam, it's going to be a hell of a lot better if you don't know all this."

"I've got to know it. Keep talking."

"All right. A man stepped into the room when Sharon opened the door. He took a card case from his pocket and identified himself as Ronley Fisher, an assistant district attorney.

"I thought it was some kind of a shakedown. Frankly, I didn't know just how to play it; whether to tell him who I was and ask him what the hell he was trying to do or wait for him to make the play. I decided to wait for him to make the play.

"Then it turned out that he was taking us at face value. He thought we were Mr. and Mrs. Carleton Blewett of San Francisco. He apologized for disturbing us but he said that he was working on a very important case and that a witness in that case was in an adjoining unit, that he thought she was going to be joined by a gentleman a little later on in the evening, that he wanted to talk with both of them. He said that he had to keep out of sight and asked if we would mind if he sat for a few minutes where he could look out the window."

"What did you tell him?"

"What could we tell him? We told him to go right ahead. We asked him if he wanted a drink. He said he didn't, so we sat there and kept up the pretense of being husband and wife from San Francisco, and a little tired."

"Then what happened?"

"Then, after about an hour, he thanked us very much, said he was ready to leave and walked out."

"Then what?"

"I thought things over, and the more I thought them over the less I liked it. I sent Sharon home in a cab. I drove my car home."

"What time?"

"Probably around two o'clock in the morning."

"Then what?"

"Then the next day I heard about Ronley Fisher being murdered. I knew that the police would check everybody who had been in that motel. I didn't know whether Fisher had told anyone about having spent some time in our unit or not. I didn't dare to take any chances. I had one person and only one person on whom I felt I could rely.

"I rang up the motel and told them I wanted to keep the unit for two more days. I sent them money for the two more days by messenger."

"Why all this trouble to keep the same unit?" I asked.

"So the police would think that the couple in it were the same people who had occupied it all along, of course."

"Then your son-in-law had never been in the place?"

"No. He only knew Sharon Barker by sight."

"How much does Sharon want out of this?"

"So far, not too much. Later on she'll want plenty."

"You'll pay?"

"I'll pay."

"What do you think happened? With Ronley Fisher, I mean."

"I don't know. I don't want to find out. I don't want to know anything about it."

"You're in a jam," I told him.

"You're not telling me anything."

"I played this thing on the up and up and got into trouble."

"How much trouble?"

"Lots of trouble."

"Your face has been scratched."

"My face has been scratched, my stomach has been punched, my jaw is sore and I spent the night in a drunk tank."

"And why are you here?"

"It's the policy of our firm to try and protect our clients, even when the clients don't disclose themselves at the start of the employment and play fair with us."

"I'm sorry," he said.

"So am I."

"What are you going to do now?" he asked.

"Try and keep you out of it if I can," I said, "but I have to know what happened."

"I've told you what happened."

"Your son-in-law had quite a story."

"I thought up the best one I could."

"The police feel I haven't been co-operating and are threatening to take my license."

"I have some political power. I can't exert it directly at this time, but when your license comes up for renewal I don't think you need to have anything to worry about."

"What about the meantime?"

"We both have things to worry about. We'll have to help each other."

Again he picked up the desk pen, and wrote out a check. He tore it off and handed it to me.

The check was for five thousand dollars.

"Spare no expense, Lam," he said, "and I'm not going to argue about your charges. This is on account for expenses and services and there'll be more."

I put the check in my pocket and shook hands.

"Can you keep me out of it?" he asked.

"I don't know," I told him. "We try to give satisfaction to our clients."

"All right," he said. "I'm your client. Remember that."

"I'm remembering," I told him, and walked to the door.

Getchell jerked the door open, raised his voice and said, "I like your style, young man. I like your initiative and your courage, but I definitely do not want to have you wasting your time and mine. Furthermore, I don't think Mr. Allen, my son-in-law, would be at all interested in your proposition. I'm not going to get mean about it this time but I don't want you to come charging in past my secretary. Do you understand?"

"Yes, sir," I said, and marched meekly out of the office.

I drove up to the courthouse as fast as I could get there.

Harcourt Parker, the trial deputy who had been selected to carry on in place of Ronley Fisher, was doing the best he could with the case.

He wasn't getting anywhere.

Staunton Cliffs was on the stand, testifying on behalf of the defense and making a good impression on the jury.

The guy was plausible, quick-witted and a good actor. He gave the impression of trying to be fair.

He was, he explained, terribly sorry that his wife had been killed. Despite the fact that they were no longer congenial and were on the point of separating, he had the greatest respect for her and esteemed her as a friend. It was simply that the old glamour had fled from the relationship.

He admitted that he had tried to spare his mistress, Marilene Curtis, from the newspaper notoriety which would inevitably result from a discovery of their relationship and therefore had lied to the police about what had happened, to the extent that he had said he and his wife were alone in their apartment at the time of the shooting.

Actually he had gone to tell his wife that he wanted a divorce and to get her to try and view the situation sensibly. He was, he said, prepared to make a very substantial property settlement.

The witness said that he had misjudged his wife, that he had felt she would recognize the inevitable, that for months there had been no normal marital relationship and he felt that she would realize the impossibility of the situation.

In place of that she had become hysterical, Cliffs said. She had grabbed a gun from a drawer and had tried to shoot Marilene Curtis, and Marilene Curtis had run from the room. The witness had grabbed his wife and asked her what in the world she was trying to do, saw she was hysterical and had slapped her hard in order to bring her to her senses. Then she had turned the gun on him and tried to shoot him, the bullet had grazed his arm, he had grabbed for the gun, she had twisted her gun hand, and in the struggle the gun had gone off and had killed her. He was sorry it had happened but he was blameless.

Cliffs was very poised and stated he was very sorry for the tragedy. He pointed out that he was a normal red-blooded man, that his wife was frigid, that she had forced him to seek companionship on the outside, that when he had finally found happiness with Marilene Curtis she had adopted a dog-in-the-manger attitude and had refused a divorce.

Marilene Curtis, the codefendant, sat with her counsel, looking up at her lover on the witness stand, at times nodding her head in confirmation of his story, at times touching her eyes with her handkerchief then elevating her chin, looking up proudly with her heart in her eyes, showing that after all she was unashamed of her love because it was normal, natural and inevitable.

The general atmosphere around the courtroom was that the best the prosecution could hope for was a hung jury, that there was no chance of a conviction, that the strong probabilities were in favor of an outright acquittal.

The witness brought his story to a dramatic conclusion.

"Cross-examine," the defense attorney said.

Parker arose and started throwing questions at the witness.

Cliffs took every question Parker threw at him and hit it over the fence for a home run. Of course Marilene Curtis was his mistress. They loved each other. They wanted to be married. They were entitled to their happiness. He had wanted his wife to consult physicians to see what could be done about her increasing frigidity. She had refused. She had long since ceased to be a wife. The rift had been the result of her own decision, and long before Marilene Curtis had come into his life. She had told him to seek outside interests. She had made a mockery of his natural desires.

Parker was getting nowhere fast, and knew it. The whole courtroom knew it. The jury knew it.

The court took a fifteen-minute recess.

I pushed my way up to Parker. "May I talk with you a moment?" I asked.

Parker looked me over. "What about?"

"About the case."

"What about it?"

"I have some information."

"That's different," he said. "Come over here. Who are you, and what do you know?"

"My name is Lam," I said. "I'm a private detective. I don't know very much but I have a hunch."

"We don't play hunches."

"I have some evidence to back the hunch."

"Go to the police with it. They investigate. I only try the cases in court."

"I've been to the police. They think I'm all wet."

"Then probably you are."

"All right," I said, "will you ask a question of the witness?"

"That depends. What is the question?"

"Ask him," I said, "if he knows Carlotta Shelton."

Parker's eyes lit up. "You mean he had an affair with her?"

"I don't know," I said. "Ask him if he knows her. Then ask him if it isn't true that he was on a party at which Carlotta Shelton and a friend of Carlotta's were present, at which the subject of his marital affairs came up for discussion. Ask him if Marilene Curtis wasn't there and if something wasn't said about killing his wife if she wouldn't give him a divorce."

Parker's eyes lit up like lights on a Christmas tree. "This you can prove?" he asked.

"No," I said. "*You* can."

He shook his head. The lights went out. "I can't even ask questions like that without having proof."

I said, "Get a continuance and I'll do something about getting proof."

"I can't get a continuance."

"How long are you going to be with your cross-examination?"

"Not very long," he said. "Frankly I'm not getting very far with this witness. They're going to have to call Marilene Curtis and I'm hoping she won't prove as good a witness as Staunton Cliffs."

"You're getting nowhere with Cliffs," I said, "and you're getting nowhere fast. Every question you ask puts him in that much more solid with the jury."

"I don't need you to tell me my business."

"You need somebody," I told him, and turned away.

"Now, wait a minute, Lam, I didn't mean to be short but I'm in a spot."

"I know you're in a spot," I said.

"And I can't ask questions like that unless I have the proof to back it up. It's unprofessional conduct to make a pass with a question like that in front of a jury."

"All right," I said, "ask him about the times he and Marilene Curtis went out together, the different places they stayed."

He threw out his hands in a gesture of surrender. "What the hell's the use? They admit it. They're proud of it. They say it was love, and there are some frustrated women on that jury who are going to put them right back in each other's arms."

"All right," I said, "you can ask him if they ever went out on a foursome, can't you?"

"Yes, I can ask that."

"Then can you ask him if he knows Carlotta Shelton?"

His eyes narrowed. "No, I don't think I can. I can't drag her name into it without—well, not unless there is some assurance that she's connected with it."

"All right," I said, "then you can lose your case and it's okay by me."

I walked away from him. This time he didn't stop me.

Court reconvened and Parker resumed his cross-examination.

By this time Cliffs knew the crisis was past. He had taken the worst that the prosecution could throw at him and he was coming off all right. He began to get flushed with victory, filled with confidence.

The tide had turned. Everyone in the courtroom sensed it. The question of a hung jury became more improbable. It looked like a certain acquittal. All Marilene Curtis had to do was to make her story stand up.

The clock crept on past eleven-thirty.

If Parker quit his cross-examination before the noon recess, he'd surrender an advantage. If he kept it up until the noon recess, he would have lost the interest, the sympathy and the attention of the jurors.

He knew it and the witness knew it.

Parker looked at the clock. "It is approaching the hour of the noon adjournment, Your Honor."

"We have twenty-five minutes left," the judge said. "Proceed."

Parker turned around toward the courtroom. He saw the faintly triumphant smile on the face of Marilene Curtis. He caught my eye. Suddenly he whirled and said to Cliffs, "Now, these parties that you went on, these surreptitious trips with Marilene Curtis, your mistress, were you always alone?"

"What do you mean? I was with Miss Curtis," Cliffs said.

"No, I mean did you ever go on a foursome with some friend of yours and another girl friend?"

Cliffs said with dignity, "Our relationship, Mr. Parker, was not one of surreptitious week-end sex dalliance. Ours was a relationship founded upon love. We would no more have included other persons in our intimacies than I would have invited another couple into my bedroom."

Parker took a deep breath. "Do you," he asked, "know Carlotta Shelton?"

The witness stiffened as though he had received a shock. "I . . . I—— Yes."

"On any of your trysts," Parker asked, "did you ever see Miss Shelton?"

"I have seen quite a few people I know from time to time. I am not——"

"Answer the question. Did you ever see Carlotta Shelton on one of your trysts?"

"I . . . I believe I did."

"Recount the circumstances of that meeting," Parker said.

"Just a minute," the attorney for the defense interposed smoothly, getting to his feet. "If the Court please, this is not proper cross-examination, and the question is not only far afield from anything that was asked on direct examination, but it calls for testimony that is incompetent, irrelevant and immaterial."

Parker said, "The witness has been describing his trysts with his mistress and the nature of them, and I am entitled to cross-examine him at length upon that subject."

"The Court is inclined to agree," the judge ruled.

"Where was I supposed to have seen her?" Cliffs asked.

"Where did you see her?"

"I had no romantic entanglement with the lady in

question, if that is what you are trying to insinuate," Cliffs said.

"I'm asking you where you saw her," Parker said.

"It is difficult to answer that question offhand. I hadn't anticipated it being asked," Cliffs said.

Parker did a grand job. He whipped a notebook out of his pocket, thumbed through the pages, then holding his thumb on one of the pages, said, "As a matter of fact you saw her several times, didn't you, Mr. Cliffs?"

Cliffs hesitated. "Well, yes . . . I believe I did."

"And on at least one of those occasions she had a boy friend with her?"

"She was usually escorted," Cliffs said. "She's a very attractive woman."

"Did you and Marilene Curtis ever ride in her automobile?"

"Yes."

"And were just the three of you in that automobile?"

"Objected to as not proper cross-examination; incompetent, irrelevant and immaterial," the defense attorney said.

"Overruled," the judge snapped.

The witness had now lost his composure. He was sweating and he was frightened.

"No," he said, "there was one other person."

"Man or woman?"

"A man."

"Miss Shelton's escort?"

"Yes."

"And where did you go on that occasion?"

"I . . . I can't remember."

"Was it out of the city?"

"I believe so, yes."

"Do you mean that you can't remember the name of the motel at which you stayed on that occasion?" Parker asked.

The defense attorney was on his feet. "Your Honor, this is incorrect, improper cross-examination. The questions call for information which is incompetent, irrelevant and immaterial. The plain attempt here is to discredit this witness by association. The only question at issue here is association of this witness with his codefendant, Marilene Curtis, and the defense has unhesitatingly admitted that and given the details of that association. It is manifestly improper to seek to arouse the prejudice of this jury by matters of association of this sort."

Parker said, "The witness has testified that he would no more think of having other persons present at the time of his trysts than he would of inviting another couple into his bedroom."

"That wasn't on direct examination, that was on cross-examination," the defense attorney said.

"I don't care when the statement was made, I have the privilege of impeaching the witness on that point," Parker insisted.

The defense attorney looked desperately at the clock. "If the Court please, it is now within a few minutes of the noon adjournment. I would like to get some authorities on this point and present them to the Court at the conclusion of the noon recess."

"Very well," the judge said. "We will at this time take our usual noon adjournment. Court will reconvene at two o'clock. During this time the members of the jury are cautioned not to form or express any opinion as to the guilt or innocence of either or both defendants, nor to discuss the case with anyone or permit it to be discussed in your presence."

The judge arose and stalked into his chambers.

Parker pushed his way through the crowd.

"Lam," he said excitedly, "I want to talk with you."

I followed him into an anteroom.

"You've struck pay dirt," he said. "That thing has

them on the run. Now, we've got to have more. We can't stop here. We've *got* to have more. You go to the police and——"

"And I'll get thrown back into the cooler," I said. "They don't like private detectives messing around in their murder cases."

"Well, what the hell *do* you want to do?"

I said, "I want you to ring up my partner, Bertha Cool. I want you to commission her as an investigator of the district attorney's office."

"And then what?"

"Then," I said, "Bertha has got to go to work on Carlotta Shelton."

"Dammit!" Parker said. "You've got me in this thing so deep now that I've *got* to go through with it."

"You were the one who brought it up," I said.

"I had to. I was licked if I didn't, and now—now I'm in one hell of a spot."

"All right," I said, "we have just a little over two hours. You can deputize me as a special investigator, which will give me some official status. You can ring up Bertha Cool on the telephone and deputize her. We'll give it a try. Our hands are tied as private investigators."

"Why the hell haven't you been working with the police?" he asked.

"Because," I said, "the police won't work with us."

He hesitated another instant, then took a long breath and said, "All right. What's Bertha Cool's telephone number?"

CHAPTER 16

WITH the facilities that Parker had at his command it took only a few minutes to find that Carlotta Shelton was out of circulation, no one knew where. The police had been making some inquiries about her in a halfhearted way.

Harden C. Monroe, prominent businessman and real estate subdivider, was out of town on business. His office was unable to tell the district attorney's office where he could be reached.

Parker looked at me.

I said, "We'll try Elaine Paisley."

"Do you think she knows where they are?"

"There are two of them," I said. "She probably knows where one of them can be reached, and———"

"All right," he interrupted. "We haven't any better lead to follow so let's go and try that."

A district attorney's chauffeur sent us through traffic with red light and siren and within exactly twelve minutes from the time we left the courthouse we were knocking on the door of Elaine Paisley's apartment.

She had on some sort of a diaphanous robe that caused the light behind her to silhouette her figure so that it was quite apparent all she had on under the filmy negligee was her own winning personality.

She fell back as we pushed our way into the apartment.

"Donald Lam!" she exclaimed. "Why, I thought——— You have no right———"

I said, "This is a man from the district attorney's office. First off we want to know where Carlotta Shelton is."

"I don't know. I haven't seen Carlotta. I don't want to see her. I can't face her."

"Why?"

"That horrid woman made me sign a statement that was false."

"What sort of a statement?"

"You know—about getting a sheet of stationery out of your desk. There's absolutely nothing to it. I wanted to see you about a highly confidential matter."

"What was it?" I asked.

This time she rattled it off glibly. "I didn't want to mention names," she said, "but I guess now I'm in a position where I have to. Harden C. Monroe is having trouble with his wife. She's been trying to frame him, and an attempt was made by private detectives to get me to swear that I'd been on a week-end trip with him."

"What did you tell them?"

"I told them that I wouldn't do anything like that. That I hardly knew Mr. Monroe. That he had talked with me about a real estate investment at one time and had always been a perfect gentleman."

"And then what?"

"And then this . . . this horrible woman came barging in and said that I hadn't had any case at all to see you about, that I only wanted to get stationery out of your office and when I denied it she threw me down on the bed and plumped herself down on my stomach.

"She knocked the wind out of me. I could hardly breathe."

I looked at Parker's face. I could see him losing enthusiasm for the whole business. I said, "Did you tell any of this to Carlotta Shelton?"

"I hardly know Carlotta Shelton. I have met Mr. Monroe in a business way, but as far as Carlotta is concerned I have been on one or two publicity stunts with her but that's all. I know her when I see her."

"You have no idea where she is now?"

"Of course not. And may I remind you *gentlemen* that

156

I was about to take my shower, that I am expecting a telegram and—well, as you can see if you have eyes, I am not dressed to receive visitors."

"All right," Parker said. "We have to locate either Monroe or Carlotta Shelton before two o'clock. Now, where's a good lead? Where could we start working?"

"I haven't the faintest idea," she said, "and I don't want to get involved in any of this. If you insist on remaining here in this apartment, I am going to have to call my attorney."

Knuckles banged on the door.

Elaine Paisley hesitated.

I opened the door.

Bertha Cool came striding into the room.

Elaine Paisley took one look at her and fell back toward the bedroom.

I said to Elaine Paisley, "Would you mind if we looked in your bedroom before we left, just to make sure no one's there?"

Then I turned to Parker and said, "This is Bertha Cool now."

Bertha Cool put her hands on her hips, stood glowering at Elaine Paisley.

"I certainly would," Elaine Paisley said. "You have no right to come in here in the first place. I didn't invite you in and you certainly can't look in my bedroom without a search warrant."

I said to Bertha, "She claims that this statement she gave you about wanting to get a sheet of stationery from the office and turning it over to Carlotta Shelton is completely phony, that you forced her to make that statement."

"Oh, is that so?" Bertha said, her diamond eyes glittering.

"And I demand that I be protected," Elaine Paisley said. "Now you gentlemen, at least one of you, represent the law. If you are from the district attorney's office I demand——"

"We'll look in your bedroom first," I said, "and then——"

She planted herself against the bedroom door, spread her arms and legs, said, "You can't go in here without a search warrant. Now, do you have a search warrant?"

Parker said, "No, we don't have a search warrant and I'm afraid we're going to have to appeal to your generosity——"

"Search warrant my fanny," Bertha said, and striding forward, jerked Elaine out of the way with one side-swiping motion of her arm, sending her spinning half across the room.

She opened the bedroom door and said, "Well, hello, Dearie. You'd better get some clothes on. There are some men out here who want to talk with you."

Elaine Paisley screamed.

Bertha walked into the bedroom. A moment later she came out with Carlotta Shelton. Carlotta was hastily pulling up the zipper on a housecoat.

"This the one you're looking for?" Bertha said.

"That's the one," I said.

Carlotta Shelton said to me, "Now look, Mr. Lam, there evidently was some misunderstanding and I want you to know that I'll make things right with you as far as that is concerned."

I said, "What I want to know right now is what happened Saturday night when you went to the Bide-a-wee-bit Motel, registered, got a unit and waited for Harden Monroe to join you. Right after he joined you, Ronley Fisher came in, identified himself and served a subpoena on you. Now, you take it from there."

"I don't know what you're talking about," Carlotta said.

"Then you damned well better find out what it's all

158

about fast," Bertha Cool said. "I'm from the district attorney's office and you're going with me."

"You can't arrest me," Carlotta Shelton said.

"The hell I can't," Bertha Cool said. "Do you want to take five minutes and get some clothes on or go the way you are?"

She turned to Elaine Paisley and said, "And as for you, you lying little bitch, you try backing up on that statement you gave me under oath and by God, I'll shake your teeth out!"

I said to Carlotta Shelton, "This is no longer just a cover-up, this is a murder case. What you do within the next five minutes determines whether you're going to be a witness or whether you're going to be put on trial for being an accessory to murder."

Bertha Cool said, "You're a good-looking bitch and you can use that body of yours to get some of the things you want out of life before you're too old to do any good with it. You spend the next ten years sitting in a women's prison, living on a starch diet, living a life of enforced celibacy and see what you look like when you come out."

Carlotta said, "It was all a terrible mistake—an accident."

"What was?" Parker asked.

"Mr. Fisher."

"You better tell us about it," I said.

She started to cry.

Bertha said, "Wipe those tears off your face, Dearie, and get started talking. We haven't got much time. These people are too smart to fall for tears and they don't mean a goddam thing to me."

Carlotta stopped crying as though she had turned a spigot somewhere and shut off the tears. She was grim, white-faced and frightened.

She said, "I don't know how Mr. Fisher found out about us. Harden Monroe and I went on a foursome with

Staunton Cliffs and Marilene. Harden knew Staunton Cliffs very well. Harden was trying to cover up because his wife was looking for evidence in a divorce case and he and Staunton Cliffs fixed up a business trip that they had to go on and then after they got started, phoned for Marilene Curtis to pick me up and bring me along."

"And what happened Saturday night?" I asked.

She said, "I went to this motel where Harden and I sometimes met and registered. After about an hour, Harden drove up and he had no sooner entered the motel unit than this man came in and identified himself as Ronley Fisher, a district attorney, and served a subpoena on us."

"Just to tell about the foursome?" I asked.

"No," she said, "about a conversation."

"What sort of conversation?"

"Staunton Cliffs was very bitter at the time we had the foursome when he and Harden had fixed up a business trip as a blind. He and Harden were talking about their women troubles, and Staunton Cliffs said his wife wouldn't give him a divorce. He said she was trying to bleed him white and get all of his property. He said that she wasn't going to do it, that he'd kill her first."

"You heard him say that?" Parker asked.

"I heard him, Marilene Curtis heard him and Harden Monroe heard him," she said wearily.

"Where and when?" Parker asked.

"It was March twenty-second at the Cactus Pear Motel."

I looked at Parker. Parker looked at his wrist watch.

Parker said to Bertha, "You're a deputy district attorney. Get some clothes on these women and get them up to court. Here's a forthwith subpoena for them to appear in court at two o'clock as witnesses for the prosecution in the case of People versus Staunton Cliffs and Marilene Curtis. Now, don't let them try anything or get together where they can have any whispered conversation."

Bertha Cool grabbed Carlotta and pushed her into the bedroom, then turned to Elaine Paisley. "Come on, Dearie," she said. "Get some clothes on and don't do any dawdling. Never mind the mascara and the rouge. You're going places and you haven't much time."

CHAPTER 17

JUDGE CRAWFORD TRENT took the bench promptly at two o'clock, said, "This is the time heretofore fixed for resuming the case of the People of the State of California versus Staunton Cliffs and Marilene Curtis. The defendants are in court, the jurors are all present. The defendant, Staunton Cliffs, was on the stand being cross-examined. You will take the stand, Mr. Cliffs."

Cliffs's attorney had been working on him during the noon hour just as a football coach works on his team between halves.

Cliffs had a lot of his confidence back as he got on the witness stand.

Parker said, "Mr. Cliffs, you have stated that you never went on a foursome with your mistress, Marilene Curtis."

"That is right."

"Do you desire to change that testimony?"

"I certainly do not."

"I am now going to ask you, Mr. Cliffs, and I want you to pay careful attention to the question, whether or not at approximately ten o'clock on the night of March twenty-second of this year at the Cactus Pear Motel in this county, where you and Harden C. Monroe had registered as the sole occupants of Unit 12, and where your codefendant, Marilene Curtis, and Carlotta Shelton had registered as the sole occupants of Unit 13, with a connecting door between the units which you had opened, and in the presence of your codefendant, Marilene Curtis, Carlotta Shelton and Harden C. Monroe, you did not state that your wife was trying to ruin you; that while she was willing to give you a divorce, she wanted a property

162

settlement which you considered unreasonable and that you'd kill her before you'd let her strip you of all your property?

"And so there can be no question of identification, I'm going to ask the bailiff to bring Carlotta Shelton into the courtroom so that the witness can see her and———"

"You don't have to," Cliffs said, talking quickly and spilling the words before he had an opportunity to think. "I didn't say it in that way. I said that my wife was trying to ruin me, just as Harden Monroe's wife was trying to ruin him, and that women of that sort were just gold diggers."

"And should be killed?" Parker said.

"I didn't say that."

"And that you would kill your wife before you would give in to her property settlement demands?"

"I may have said that women like that should be killed, but I certainly didn't say I was going to kill her."

"Did you say that you'd like to kill her?"

"I—I had been drinking and I was angry. I . . . I don't know what I said."

"You don't remember what you said?"

"Frankly I do not."

"You were drunk at the time?"

"I had been drinking."

"So then you may have said that you would kill your wife before you would let her strip you of your property."

"I don't remember."

"And you had previously testified in this court that you would no more consider taking another party with you on your love trysts than you would think of inviting a couple of friends into your bedroom. Do you now wish to change that testimony?"

"I . . . I had forgotten about this occasion," Cliffs said wearily.

"So that you not only did go on a foursome, but the

occasion made so little impression on your mind that you had forgotten all about it."

"I—— It wasn't that it failed to make an impression on my mind."

"But you had forgotten about it?"

"Well, there had been so many times . . ."

"So many times you had been on foursomes?" Parker asked.

"Well, Monroe and I were both having domestic troubles. We had some business deals together and occasionally we would manufacture a business situation so that we could leave together and then we would be joined by—by the others."

"Oh, so then there was more than one occasion that you had been on foursomes with Harden Monroe and Carlotta Shelton."

"Yes."

"And you had forgotten about all of them?"

"I . . . I couldn't recall the various circumstances at the moment."

"So you said that you had *never* been on a foursome, in your testimony."

"Yes."

"That was false?"

"That was false."

"You were lying?"

"Yes, I was lying."

"Under oath," Parker said.

"Yes!" Cliffs screamed at him.

Parker bowed to the judge. "If the Court please, that concludes my cross-examination."

The judge looked down at the attorneys.

"That concludes the defendant's case on behalf of Staunton Cliffs," one of the lawyers said.

"How about Marilene Curtis?" Judge Trent asked.

The other lawyer arose. "If the Court please, while we

164

had assured the Court that Marilene Curtis would take the witness stand in her own behalf, we have now decided to rest the case on the evidence before the Court. The defendant, Marilene Curtis, rests."

"Any rebuttal?" Judge Trent asked.

"Yes, I wish to call Carlotta Shelton and I will state to the Court that we are making a determined effort to have a forthwith subpoena served upon Harden Monroe. However, the examination of Miss Shelton will probably take all afternoon, including as it does a statement which may well throw some light upon the death of my late associate, Ronley Fisher."

The courtroom buzzed into an uproar.

Judge Trent said, "The Court at this time will take a ten-minute recess."

CHAPTER 18

WE SAT in the office of the district attorney, who was beaming all over his face.

Parker was trying to appear modest and retiring, but not making a very good job of it.

The newspaper reporters had had their interviews and had left.

An attendant opened the door and said, "Sergeant Sellers is here."

"Show him in," the district attorney said.

Sellers came in. The district attorney regarded him in frowning appraisal.

"Sergeant," he said, "I sent for you because I wanted to make myself perfectly plain.

"We have, as you are aware, obtained convictions in the case of Staunton Cliffs and Marilene Curtis, but what is more to the point, we have solved the mystery surrounding the death of my deputy, Ronley Fisher.

"It seems that Fisher developed information which led him to serve a subpoena late Saturday night on Carlotta Shelton and Harden C. Monroe.

"Monroe was engaged in a property settlement deal with his wife and felt that any testimony which would have given his wife an opportunity to strip him of his property would be most disadvantageous. He had an argument with Fisher, followed Fisher out of the unit in the motel, and they moved over toward the telephone· booth where Fisher was going to make a call.

"While they were engaged in angry expostulation, Monroe lost his temper and took a swing at Fisher. Fisher hit back. The lock on the rear gate was broken in the struggle.

166

Monroe forced Fisher back through the broken gate. Fisher made a swing, Monroe sidestepped, Fisher lost his footing and fell into what he doubtless felt was a pool and expected he would be none the worse for his experience than a wetting. Actually the pool was empty and he took a ten-foot plunge down to the solid concrete.

"Thereafter, there was an elaborate attempt at covering up on the part of all concerned.

"This office feels that it owes a very great debt of gratitude to the firm of Cool and Lam, private investigators, who have temporarily been made assistant investigators to the district attorney's office."

Sellers simply nodded.

"I feel," the district attorney went on, "that if there had been a little more co-operation on your part, the case could have been disposed of earlier and perhaps in a less dramatic manner. I don't want the people of this community to think that the district attorney's office is deliberately courting dramatic developments such as occurred in court during the last minutes of the trial of Staunton Cliffs and Marilene Curtis. But I do want the people of this county to realize that we are fighters who never give up and who are indefatigable in our investigations."

Sellers nodded wearily.

"I note," the district attorney went on, "that there is some question about how it happened Donald Lam spent a night in the drunk tank—a most unfortunate experience. However, he feels that there was probably some genuine mistake, and has suggested that this office forget it. I thought that you should know that."

Again Sellers nodded.

"And," the district attorney went on, "Donald Lam tells me that when he was taken into custody on a suspicion of blackmail, one thousand dollars was taken from his hip pocket; a thousand dollars in numbered bills. That money was taken from his personal possession. It was impounded as evidence on a charge that was to be placed against him, but it appears that the person who was to be the prosecuting witness not only has no desire to place such a charge, but that the entire charge itself was completely trumped up."

Sellers said, "You feel that Lam is entitled to the one thousand dollars?"

"It was taken from his possession," the district attorney said.

Sellers said, "And Lam is not going to press any charges against the police on account of that unfortunate experience in the drunk tank?"

"So I understand," the district attorney went on. "I was going to suggest that in view of the fact, and since the firm of Cool and Lam seem to be very high-class investigators, the police should co-operate with them wherever possible instead of trying to make things difficult for them.

"In fact, if you had listened a little more carefully to Lam, there is no doubt but that *you* could have had the credit of solving the mystery surrounding Fisher's death, instead of having that matter cleared up in a very dramatic highlight in the courtroom this afternoon by one of my deputies."

Sellers gulped, got up, came over to me and shook hands. "Thanks, Lam," he said.

He went over and shook hands with Bertha Cool. "You can count on all the co-operation I can give you," he said.

He turned to the district attorney. "That's what you wanted?"

"That's what I wanted," the district attorney said.

"*And* the thousand dollars," I reminded Sellers.

>>> If you've enjoyed this book and would like to discover more great vintage crime and thriller titles, as well as the most exciting crime and thriller authors writing today, visit: >>>

The Murder Room
Where Criminal Minds Meet

themurderroom.com